Shorty Bean
and the
Coin of Fire

The Mystery R

by

Holly K. Szurpicki

Shorty Bean and the Coin of Fire
Copyright © 2011—Holly K. Szurpicki

ISBN: 978-0-9992323-2-3

Library of Congress Control Number: 2011918854
Szurpicki, H. K. ,1976 -

Text Design: Lisa Simpson, Simpson Productions
llustrations by NeKeysha Guyton

DaShawn L. Hall- Director
Front & Back Cover by NeKeysha Guyton

Dedication

I would like to thank God for giving me the ability to make this happen.

I would like to thank my children Jonathon and Colleen who light my life with love and laughter.

To my dearest Husband John and my delightful nieces and nephews.

I would like to thank my Mother who has supported me with prayer and great excitement.

And special thanks to my illustrator NeKeysha Guyton, and DaShawn L. Hall of Manneristic Studios, Erica Hubert, Mary Knox-Johnson and Karen Hardin for editing support.

Table of Contents

Introduction

It's Christmas! And this year, Shorty Bean will be performing in a Christmas play at her school! But what will happen after the Christmas play once all of the students are dismissed for winter break is where the real adventure begins. Shorty Bean and her parents will go to her grandparent's cottage for Christmas. But Shorty had no way of knowing that it would launch a series of events which would bring unexpected change as lives are forever rearranged.

Shorty Bean often reflected to the last time she was at her grandparents and how the Coin of Fire fell from her hands into the depths of the river. It was a dreadful day on that mountain top with White Cloud and Smarty. But anytime she is at her grandparent's the ordinary becomes rather extraordinary and what Shorty didn't know was that a profound mystery had begun to stir in the deepest parts of the forest as new creatures immerged. Unexpected characters had moved into the oak tree at the cottage and under the deck where Mrs. Patty lives along with some new visitors.

As Shorty Bean packed for the trip, she fondly remembered her dearest friends she met the last time she was in the enchanted forest. Wonderful friends like White Cloud, Tripod, Sir Davy, Ms. Nora and Ben-Jeer, just to name a few.

Shorty Bean and the Coin of Fire is about

a place of light,

And a victory won in the darkest night.

Which can only be seen through the eyes

of a little girl's sight,

As her imagination takes flight.

Chapter One

Merry Christmas

S horty Bean could best be described as an imaginative and spunky girl. She had a cherished best friend named Smarty. For lack of a better word, he could be called a ham dog of sorts. What that meant was he was part dog and well, part hamster. He could always make Shorty Bean smile with his delightful face and his witty ways. The two did everything together. Well almost. He couldn't go to school with her, but each day he would wait expectantly at the door until his friend returned home and they could enjoy more adventures together like the last one they encountered. It had placed them face to face with a forest full of unusual characters—some kind and some dangerous—who helped them discover a heart locket which contained golden coins which held divine power.

Shorty frowned. But the set was not complete. One coin eluded them which was the Coin of Fire. She had held it in her hand! But now that it was gone, the mystery could not be revealed until it was discovered once again.

Shorty Bean tapped her foot unconsciously to the Christmas music playing in her room as she let her mind wander. The Christmas play was just a few days away and then it was off to her grandparents where they would celebrate Christmas AND her birthday which just happened to fall on Christmas day! She could not wait to get back to their cottage which was a place of imagination and wonder.

She reached down to pet Smarty who was snuggled against her. His red cape, which he wore everywhere, was now covered with patches. Each patch marked their adventures in forest. Last year, while Shorty Bean visited her grandparent's cottage, Grandma Ellie helped her sew patches onto Smarty's cape. Shorty Bean's eyes sparkled as she looked at the hand sewn memories. She closed her eyes for a moment as she envisioned all her forest friends. "I cannot wait to go back to the cottage," she said to Smarty. He nodded in agreement. He liked to go there as much as Shorty did!

But that was still a few days away. First, they had to decorate their home for Christmas and then it would be time for her school's Christmas play. Once she finished packing, Shorty got up to go downstairs in search of the Christmas decorations. She was alone in the house as her parents had been extremely busy volunteering and organizing supplies for local charities in their community.

Shorty located some of the tubs of Christmas decorations and began to hang the wreaths and tie bows onto their bannister. Christmas time in the city had its own special feeling. Residents decorated their homes with wreaths, garland, and beautiful bows. The city display sparkled with the colors of gold, silver, purple and green and Christmas wreaths hung down from the tops of carriage lanterns. As Shorty tied off one of the bows, she heard her parent's key in the lock of the front door and then saw it push open.

"We're home, honey! Come look at the Christmas lights, outside!" her mother called.

"Coming, Mom, coming!" Shorty Bean replied as she scooped up Smarty and raced for the door.

"It's beautiful!" she exclaimed as she looked out over the glowing beauty. It was light a fairy land. There were candy-coated berries and streams of lavender ribbons that graced the streets and candles glowed from the windows of many of the shops. It was enchanting.

"Okay, let's go in. It's time to decorate *our* home and tree," Shorty's dad exclaimed as they turned to go inside. Shorty Bean, Smarty, Mom, and Dad gather around their tree. It was about seven feet tall and just waiting to be decorated.

"Hand me the red button ornament," Dad said. Shorty Bean raised up on her tip toes and placed the ornament in her Dad's outstretched hand. Slowly the tree filled up with beautiful antique ornaments and strings of popcorn balls.

Shorty Bean placed a couple of silver ornaments along Smarty's tail. He pranced about as he wagged his tail, swinging it so he could pass the ornaments back to Shorty Bean. It was like a form of catch. Having a ham dog as a pet was awesome! Smarty helped her with everything.

Dad laughed, as Smarty displayed his goofy grin. In no time at all they were done with the tree. Shorty Bean and Smarty plopped down on the couch to relax and enjoy their handiwork. "Have some hot chocolate," Mom said as she handed both Shorty and Dad a steaming mug.

"Mmmmmm. It's yummy! Thanks, Mom," Shorty said with a smile.

Mom sat down on the sofa with them and they all cuddled ever so close to admire the decorations. Dad tried to stifle a big yawn, but was unsuccessful.

"It's time for bed. It's been a long day," he declared as he stood.

"Can I stay up for a little while and look at the Christmas tree, please?" Shorty Bean begged giving her Dad her best big-eyed look. She knew he couldn't resist her.

"Okay, just a little while longer though and then to bed," he stated as she bent down so he could kiss her on the head.

"I'm heading to bed as well, sweetie," said her Mom as she kissed her on the cheek and stood to join Dad. "Be sure to turn off the lights when you head to bed."

As her parents left the room they dimmed the lights. All alone, Shorty whispered to Smarty, "This is a wonderful life. Don't you think so?" The living room radiated with light from the fire blazing in the hearth. Smarty nodded his head and licked Shorty Bean's face. "Do you have to go outside, Smarty?"

In response, Smarty jumped off the sofa and headed to the door for his before bed bathroom break. Shorty Bean opened the door for him and he rushed out. But instead of doing his business, he started digging in the snow down to the grass.

"Smarty!! Shorty hollered. "Hurry up!"

Of course, it was cold outside, and although snow covered the grass, the ground itself was still not completely frozen. Smarty marked his turf. It was, 'a territorial thing.' He dug his paws down into the snow kicking the white powder behind him. Once the grass appeared a tiny tick crawled up his hind leg blending in perfectly with his fur.

It is common for ticks to sneakily mount their unsuspecting hosts. They are super sleuths and can easily go undetected. Most ticks come from heavily wooded areas and it was odd that this one survived within the city limits. This was no ordinary tick, because if he was he would be hibernating by now or even dead because of the frigid temperatures. He had rabbit ear antennas on top of his head and his name was Norm, Norm the tick. It certainly was no coincidence he was at that exact spot on the front lawn at the most divine hour.

Smarty shivered, shaking back and forth and then hurried back inside to warm himself by the smoldering fire. He curled up on the red braided rug in front of the hearth. Shorty Bean was snuggled up on the sofa. Her eyes heavy as the warmth of the room crept over her. She was soon asleep. That's when something extraordinary began to happen for it was Christmas time—the season of miracles!

Above the fireplace mantel, a faint image began to glow. It was shimmering gold in the shape of a circle with a blue flame radiating from the center. It was the Coin of Fire! Smarty recognized the image from their adventure the previous summer before it had disappeared. The Coin of Fire contained a power given only to those who believe. And when faith was mixed with its power, it made the locket clasped around Shorty Bean's neck glow and it strengthened her faith.

Smarty watched as smoke from the fireplace slithered up to the coin of fire, circling the surface of the coin. Smarty watched in amazement as the smoke seemed to form into a hand which began to paint the coin with a brush of fire.

Frantic, Smarty raced to Shorty Bean and jumped up and down on her stomach. He had to wake her up. He licked her face and pulled her ears, but she didn't stir. He couldn't wake her! Just then a beam of light shot out of the coin. It lifted Smarty up into the air and twirled him around in slow motion. Terrified, he reached for Shorty Bean, but nothing seemed to wake her.

Suddenly, Shorty Bean rubbed her eyes and sat up. "Is this a dream?" she asked as the light from the coin disappeared.

Smarty looked closely into Shorty Bean's eyes. He had to tell her an image of the Coin of Fire had just appeared! "Wee, da, da, Muuus ttt eee," he stuttered trying his best to communicate.

"What? Smarty!" What a miracle it was for since Smarty was born he could not speak at all. The only way Shorty and Smarty could communicate was through sign language.

Tears filled Shorty Bean's eyes. Her friend was trying to talk to her. "Smarty, it is okay. You can tell me. What's going on?"

"We must go back," Smarty finally pushed out. Shorty Bean was astounded as she heard Smarty's first words. But what did he mean?

"Go back where?"

"Back to the Gazman Forest, and also to the Caves of Rain. There is a treasure there. I cannot explain it, but I will know when I see it, Trust me!" Smarty replied. It was all he could get out for now. He wanted to tell her an image of the coin had just appeared above the mantle. That a beam of light had lifted him up in the air, and that her necklace had lit up like the Christmas tree. But for now, it would have to do.

Shorty Bean looked at her friend and realized something important must have happened. Could this be part of the mystery revealing itself? They both knew the Coin of Fire contained a power truly amazing and not of this world. Perhaps it was responsible for Smarty's ability to speak for the first time?

"By the way, when you tie my cape around my neck, it is too tight." Smarty stated.

"You mean you held back all this time in telling me?" Shorty Bean said with a laugh. "I am very sorry! Here, let me fix it for you," Shorty exclaimed as she reached up to untie the cape and loosen its hold. As Shorty Bean started to tie the cape, she pulled the clasp even snugger.

"Very funny, Shorty," Smarty said with a cough barely able to catch his breath.

Shorty Bean bursts out laughing as she loosened the strap and gently untied his cape.

"It's time for bed. We can make sure we get it right tomorrow," she stated as she headed for the stairs. Smarty wasn't tired any longer. In fact, he was rather exhilarated regarding his new voice and began to whistle through his front teeth.

"Smarty, hush, you will wake up Mom and Dad!" Shorty said with a giggle as they reached her bedroom. She opened the door and Smarty leapt in front and raced into the room. He burrowed into a pair of animal slippers near the bed, turned around and poked his head out.

Suddenly, Smarty felt uneasy. There was a presence of someone else in the room. Who could it be Shorty knew Smarty well and could tell he was uneasy, the fur on his back was raised. "It's probably nothing," she thought to herself as she wiggled under her covers. Soon they were both fast asleep.

Like almost every other night, Shorty Bean began to dream about the heart locket as it glowed on her neck and unveiled the secret places of the forest. She wondered would she ever see her friends in the forest? Would they still be there? She thought of her special friends like Ms. Nora, Tripod, White Cloud, Sir Davy, and Ben-Jeer? She could only imagine where they were and what they were doing now.

The sun was shining through her windows when Shorty Bean awoke. It was time for school. Smarty had managed to crawl into bed without her knowing it. He stuck his head out from under the covers, but remained still. Shorty Bean crawled out of bed and looked at herself in her mirror. Her hair was sticking out everywhere! Today was her school play and nothing was going to stop her. Crazy hair or not she had a play to get to!

Smarty found her morning hair quite amusing. "Smarty, Stop it!" she insisted. In response Smarty just laughed. Shorty tried to brush her hair back into place as she looked into the mirror. That's when she noticed Smarty had jumped out of bed, leapt down the hallway to the bathroom and was brushing his teeth with *her* toothbrush!

"YUCK, that is totally disgusting! It's just plain gross," she shouted stomping down the hallway to grab it from his sneaky paws. Norm the tick peeked out from Smarty's fur, his antennas raised, but no one seemed to notice him.

Smarty had a thing for Shorty's toothbrush. It fascinated him how it seemed to grow when water was added to it. "Relax, will yaw?" Smarty stated.

Then a voice echoed, "Relax will yaw?

"What was that?" Smarty questioned as he looked around the room.

"What was that?" the voice said again.

"You're going to be late for school!" Smarty announced as he looked at his watch.

"You're going to be late for school!" the voice echoed.

"Who is that?" Shorty asked as she bent down close to Smarty to check his fur.

"I don't know, I am wondering the same thing!" Smarty replied.

Shorty looked Smarty over, but she saw nothing. Norm had managed to elude them again! He was sneaky. Even though they tried, they were unable to uncover the identity of the mysterious voice. Shorty Bean was close, but not close enough.

"You know, I am not sure if I can get used to you talking to me," Shorty said with a laugh before she exclaimed, "Oh, no! You're right; I have to go now!" she exclaimed. The Christmas play is this afternoon and I can't be late! About that time Dad yelled up the stairs, "Shorty, Shorty, hurry up! You're going to be late for school! Smarty raced up her arm and shoulder to her head where he straightened her headband. He then gave her a hug and kissed her on the cheek.

Shorty Bean started to sign to Smarty, but caught herself and put her hands in her pocket. Shorty Bean and Smarty ran down the stairs together. She grabbed her book back and raced out the door, but not before she grabbed her coat. It was cold outside!

After Shorty Bean left for school, Smarty pranced back up to the bedroom, grinning all the way. He sprang onto the bed, curled his tail around his body and closed his eyes.

Within seconds he was snoring ever so loudly. Norm accompanied him and it was like hearing a snoring symphony.

Chapter Two

The School Play

Shorty Bean raced to the drama class as soon as the bell rang for the day. Tonight, was the annual Christmas play. As the head elf she would get to sing and dance. She pulled out her costume to work on finishing touches as her classmates filed into the room and chatter filled the air. The students who didn't get parts were just as busy cutting out green paper ears for the elf costumes.

"An hour to go, get in your costumes," the drama teacher announced as she walked through the auditorium inspecting costumes, lighting and design. Shorty Bean donned her costume and then pulled out a red and white sparkle marker to paint knee-high striped tights on her legs.

"Shorty, that looks wonderful!" her teacher exclaimed! Is everything else finished?" she asked.

"Yes, ma'am, all except painting my daisy toe ring. It will be my masterpiece," Shorty said with a grin. Shorty Bean's daisy toe ring was very important to her. No matter what the occasion, the daisy toe ring always received the most delicate care and attention. Tonight, she would paint each petal green and red and then when it dried she would glue red holly berries on the tip of each petal. Just as she finished the delicate task one of her friends can running through the room and plopped down beside Shorty Bean.

"Hey, you almost made me spill my paint!" Shorty declared. But she couldn't stay mad at her friend.

"I'm sorry, but I just peeked through the stage curtains and the auditorium is beginning to fill up! And I just saw your parents come in. They are on the second row right in the center!

Suddenly Shorty felt like she had butterflies in her stomach. They began to dance and flutter about. She rubbed her hands on her costume to dry them and looked in the mirror. She was ready!

"Can you believe our Shorty Bean is the lead elf? I'm so proud of her," her mom said as she checked her camera video. She wanted to catch every bit of it!

The overhead lights dimmed, and the curtains slowly opened. When it was with time for Shorty Bean's part she stepped onto the stage. It felt warm with all the lights and then the spot light found her, and she felt sweat begin to trickle down her face. Suddenly she felt those butterflies in her stomach flit around again, but plunged ahead as she grasped the microphone firmly and began to sing, "It's Christmas time, and father time, has come a new beginning. I see your face. Oh, how it glows. I cannot keep from singing, nothing in between, or even as it seems, but now I know the meaning. It's Christmas time."

Shorty finished her song without a hitch. At least to her it seemed the play had just started when it was over. The cast all returned to the stage and took a bow. The audience burst into applause and Shorty's mom and dad cheered loudly, "Bravo, Bravo!" they yelled. Shorty Bean smiled. She could hear her parents above the roar and loved having the support of her family and friends.

After all the congratulations, Shorty Bean and her family headed back home. Now that the play was over, and school dismissed for Christmas break, they would soon be heading to her grandparents.

Once they arrived home, the first thing Shorty Bean did was look for Smarty. She ran up to her bedroom and called out, "Smarty, I missed you, where are you?" Startled awake from a comfy spot on her bed, He blinked and then laughed. "What are you laughing at?" Shorty Bean asked as she pet his pointy head. Then she caught her reflection in the mirror and had to giggle herself. She was still wearing the green pointy elf ears!

"Get ready for bed, sweet heart," Shorty's mom said as she and her dad entered Shorty's room. "Tomorrow we are leaving early to go visit Grandpa Andy and Grandma Ellie," she finished.

"You did a great job tonight, honey! We are so proud of you!" her dad added as he kissed her goodnight.

"Goodnight, Mom and Dad. I love you, too, and thank you," Shorty Bean replied as she hugged them both. The energy that had been pent up all day was now gone and Shorty Bean was suddenly very tired. She took off her green paper ears and placed them on the dresser. Smarty pointed his paw and laughed again, but Shorty Bean chose to have selective hearing and ignored him. She smiled to herself. She'd show him!

Crawling into bed, she pulled the comforter up over her shoulders and snuggled into the sheets until they grew warm. Smarty jumped up on the bed and curled up next to her pillow. Within a minute they were both fast asleep.

In the middle of the night after a quick bathroom break, Shorty Bean put her plan into action. She tiptoed over to her dresser and gently picked up the green paper ears. She opened the dresser drawer slowly, as she tried to not make any noise. She felt around in the darkness for her bottle of glue. Ah ha, there it was! With glue in one hand and the green paper ears in the other, she quietly tiptoed back over to Smarty and gently pasted the green paper ears to his head.

"We will see who's laughing now," Shorty whispered to herself trying hard not to laugh. She loved Smarty, but also wanted to teach him a valuable lesson. That making fun of anyone, especially a best friend, is not polite!

"Shorty get up and get moving! We're going to leave in an hour," her mother called up to her from downstairs. Shorty quickly jumped up and out of bed and walked to the dresser to decide what she would wear. Her mother's voice had awakened Smarty as well. He jumped down from the bed and wobbled down the hallway to the bathroom. Shorty worked hard to keep a straight face as if nothing was different and resisted the urge to follow him. But she knew it wouldn't take long…

Smarty jumped up onto the sink. But when he saw himself in the mirror, he screamed! "Eeek!" he shouted.

A loud THUD followed as Smarty fell over. But no matter how Smarty shook his head back and forth trying to remove the green paper ears they stayed firmly in place. Smarty was not particularly pleased. In the bedroom, Shorty Bean belly laughed.

"Thanks a lot. I look ridiculous!" Smarty announced as he stomped into the room. Shorty Bean tried her best to contain her laughter as she responded to her distressed friend.

"No, no, Smarty, you don't look ridiculous, you look adorable," Shorty Bean exclaimed and truly meant it. Shorty stuck out his upper lip and wiggled his nose. Shorty Bean wrapped her arms around him and kissed him on the head. "I was just having fun. I am sorry. I didn't mean to hurt your feelings!" she told him as she chuckled. There was just something about those big green ears on his small head that made her feel jolly! But instead of staying angry, Smarty started laughing, too. It was a pretty funny joke and he deserved it after laughing at her. Besides, it's always better to laugh *with* someone than laugh *at* someone.

Shorty slung her backpack over her shoulder and grabbed her suitcase and then picked Smarty up in her other arm. She turned off her light and they headed downstairs.

"Here's my suitcase, Dad," Shorty said as she set it down beside her dad who was at the car trying to get everything packed.

"There is enough luggage in this trunk as if we were going away for three months," her Dad complained as he shoved a bag over to make room for Shorty's suitcase.

"Well, you'll have to make room, I have one more bag still upstairs," her mother said with a giggle as she ran inside to get it.

"Now, Shorty, that rat is not going with us on vacation and I mean it!" her dad stated. Shorty was horrified. She couldn't leave him! It was a known fact that Dad didn't care for pets, but he knew how much Smarty meant to Shorty Bean and that was enough for him to allow Smarty into the family. He preferred not to travel with him though. Smarty tended to shed fluffy hairs and heat and flying hair don't mix. It would fair up his allergies and cause him to sneeze violently as it launched his glasses onto the dashboard of the car.

"Dad please? I promise he won't even make a sound," she begged. Smarty peered up at Shorty Bean as if to say something, but she signed to him to keep quiet, placing her finger over her mouth.

Just then Shorty's mom came back out of the house with the last suitcase. "This is it! I think we are ready to go," she declared as dad made room for it in the trunk. As he clicked it shut, Shorty and Smarty jumped into the car. "Stay down and stay quiet!" Shorty told Smarty. I don't want to have to leave you!

Dad seemed to have forgotten Smarty as he slid into the driver's seat and started the engine. But it wasn't until they pulled onto the interstate that Shorty Bean breathed a sigh of relief that Smarty had been able to come. Her dad and Smarty weren't exactly the best of friends, but she didn't think her dad would really make her leave her friend all alone at Christmas! Shorty Bean rolled down her window and breathed in the smell of the tall pines. It was like breathing in a little bit of heaven. She listened as the wipers hummed across the windshield to clear it from the rain and Shorty let her mind wander to the wonderful day ahead.

Smarty, finally assured he wasn't going to be left behind emerged and stuck his head out the window. He did so just as Dad hit a large puddle, causing dirty water to splash up on his face. Smarty bonked his head as he jerked his head back in the window. Dad chuckled even as Mom elbowed him in the side and gave him a look of disapproval.

"Oh, my!" Shorty Bean exclaimed as she used her shirt sleeve to wipe Smarty's goggles and face from the water. Smarty decided to crawl back into her backpack. It might be safer if he just stayed inside there for a while!

Chapter Three

Winter Vacation

"That's a lovely song," Shorty Bean whispered to Smarty as a soft melody reached her ears.

"It's not me," Smarty whispered back.

"It's not me," a voice echoed. It was Norm the tick. They had still not discovered him! He chuckled to himself.

Shorty Bean was extremely confused. "Where could the voice be coming from?" she wondered. It wasn't her mom or dad and the radio wasn't on either. Smarty lifted his head out of the backpack and cocked his head to listen. They both heard the voice, but neither could figure out where it came from.

"Are we there yet?" Shorty Bean asked from the back seat.

Her father held back the sigh it was clear he was frustrated. How many times had Shorty asked that in the last thirty minutes?

"Have patience, Shorty, there's no need to hurry. We'll be there soon," her father responded.

Shorty Bean let out a big sighed. "All right, Daddy. I'm just excited." Shorty turned her head to gaze out the window again hoping to pass the time. This time of the year the winding road leading to her grandparents 'cottage was adorned with diamond snow. It clung to the trees, bushes and everything around. The ice crystals covered everything like a blanket that sparkled making it look like a winter wonderland.

"Look, Shorty, a deer," her dad exclaimed as he pointed toward one of the homes. Shorty quickly looked in the direction of her dad's pointed arm and saw there were indeed two deer in someone's yard. But there was only one problem. They were made of plastic!

"Dad, those are not real," Shorty Bean exclaimed. Her dad burst out laughing at his joke. Shorty Bean shook her head. "Parents, what can you do with them?" Shorty whispered to Smarty.

As they turned down the drive to her grandparent's home, Shorty admired the snow perched on the top of each pine tree. It looked like fluffy cotton balls. Her dad pulled into the circular driveway and turned off the motor. They had arrived! As she climbed out of the car, Shorty noticed that Grandma Ellie and Grandpa Andy had decorated. There were candy apple red holly berries draped down from the window boxes and a large red and white candy cane hanging from the door knob. Two rows of miniature Christmas trees graced the walkway leading up to the front door and a small sign read, "Welcome" near the mailbox. A whitish blue smoke floated from the chimney signaling that Grandpa Andy had started a fire for them. Oh, how she loved being back at the cottage!

Grandpa Andy opened the door when he heard their footsteps on the porch. He folded Shorty into a big bear hug and then reached for her parents. Shorty fingered her heart shaped locket around her neck as she entered their cottage. She breathed in the aroma of gingerbread cookies, one of Grandma Ellie's specialties. The cottage was just as she remembered, full of charm with picture frames that adorned the walls. Each one filled with memories telling stories of years gone by.

"I see everyone made it safely! How was the traffic? I heard there were some issues up north," Grandma Ellie said as she gave each one a kiss. From the corner of Shorty Bean's eye, she noticed an unusual chair in the living room by the bay window. It hadn't been there during the summer.

"Whose chair is that, Grandpa?" Shorty asked as she walked over to the small piece of furniture.

"I made it especially for Smarty," he replied with a twinkle in his eyes. Shorty noticed a tiny hook on the side of the chair to hang Smarty's adventure cape. It was perfect!

Smarty swaggered past her dad and jumped up on his new chair. He grinned from ear to ear as if to say, "What do you think of me now?" Smarty loved the attention he received from Grandpa Andy.

"Smarty flipped his cape over his shoulder as he sat on his new chair. He felt regal and stuck his nose in the air as he relished his new position.

"Are you kidding me? Who is that, King Smarty? Really, Dad. His very own chair? Give me a break!" Dad exclaimed.

Grandpa rocked back on his heels and grinned. Shorty's dad brought the suitcases in and after they were all settled, Grandma Ellie whispered in Shorty Bean's ear. "I have missed you so much my dear. Would you like some hot tea and milk?"

Shorty Bean nodded, "Sure! I would love some. May I have a few gingerbread cookies too?"

"Of course, you may," said Grandma Ellie. "I made them special for you."

Over cookies and milk, Shorty Bean and Grandma Ellie reminisced about all the adventures from the past. Time seemed to fly as they sat around the fire and talked. Shorty's eyes grew heavy realized just how tired she truly was. "Grandma Ellie, may I go on upstairs to my bedroom? I'm tired. Do you think when you are finished in the kitchen you can pray with me?"

"Yes, of course, my dear," Grandma Ellie replied.

Shorty Bean got up and started to walk past Grandpa Andy who was sitting in his green leather chair reading the newspaper. It was then that she got a burst of energy and raced past him.

"Slow down and walk," he instructed. "Goodnight, little one. How about another hug before bed?"

Shorty Bean wrapped her arms around her Grandpa and planted a kiss on his cheek. Then she and Smarty headed upstairs to the bedroom.

"Excuse me, I burped," Smarty exclaimed as they got ready for bed.

"Your breath smells gross, yuck, it really stinks!" Shorty Bean said.

"I had some tea and milk," he replied as he covered his mouth with his paw. He took his cape off and carefully folded it as Shorty took off her heart locket and laid it on the little table next to the bed waiting for Grandma Ellie to pray with them.

Chapter Four

𝒯uck me in

A s she climbed into bed, Shorty Bean heard Grandma Ellie's footsteps on the creaky stairway. She opened the door and walked to the bed to tuck Shorty in bed. Grandma Ellie smiled as she gently petted the top of Smarty's head and brushed Shorty's bangs out of her eyes. She picked up an extra blanket to cover them both up. Once they were both snuggled in, she knelt beside the bed folded her hands and began to pray.

"Night falls and the sky begins to sleep. I pray the Lord your soul to keep. I know that angels will be sitting nearby, to watch you at night and fly, fly, fly. Tuck yourself in bed my dear and dream of candies and elephant ears, and think about what daybreak will bring, when we spend the day together and watch the morning shine and sing. May God bless us everyone, the skies, the oceans, the seasons, and the sun. Bless mommies and daddies and little girls, too and Smarties and Grandpas and Grandmas too. And help us to always remember you, you, you. Amen," Grandma Ellie concluded softly.

Shorty Bean opened her eyes to see Dad and Mom are standing directly behind Grandma Ellie. As they both bent down to kiss Shorty Bean on her forehead, her dad noticed Smarty. "Get that rat off the bed!" he raised his voice.

Smarty crawled off the bed onto the cold wooden floor mumbling under his breath, "Some people should just leave me alone!" Smarty's mumbling voice echoed in the silent room.

"Did you hear that?" Mom asked. Shorty Bean remained silent. She wasn't going to say anything.

"Hear what?" Dad asked. "Goodnight, sleep well; I love you," he said to Shorty as he walked out of the room.

"I love you, too, Mom and Dad," Shorty responded as her Mom also exited and closed the door behind her.

The minute they were gone, Smarty jumped back up on the bed. "Good, they're gone," he said with a huff.

"I heard that!" her dad hollered. Smarty flew off the bed again onto the bedroom floor. He hid under the bed where he quivered and shivered. Shorty Bean had already fallen asleep by the time he had the courage to creep out of his hiding place. But he wasn't tired anymore! So, he crept part way down the stairs and slid his head through the banister to watch. He went undetected by Mom and Dad, Grandpa Andy, and Grandma Ellie. He didn't want to miss any of the Christmas celebration.

Shorty watched as Grandma Ellie and Grandpa Andy danced in the firelight and while Mom and Dad sang. Soon they were reminiscing as they shared memories and special times they had spent together at the cottage. As the photo albums come out, Grandpa Andy put on some of his old vinyl records. They began to sing along with the old tunes. It felt very nostalgic to listen to artists from the past, reflecting on a different generation. But Smarty couldn't help himself and burst out in laughter. It was a dreadful display of late night karaoke for not one of them could carry a note!

Mrs. Patty the blind old cat who lived under the deck, in the backyard gazed in the dining room window from outside with her paws on the window pane as she smiled and wagged her fluffy tail back and forth in rhythm with the music.

Smarty chuckled and as he did he accidentally bumped his head on the side of the bannister.

"I keep hearing someone laughing," Dad stated.

"You're silly Bud," Mom said. Shorty Bean is asleep. You must be tired. Smarty grew quiet, so that Dad would not notice him and crept quietly back upstairs to the bedroom.

A few hours later, Shorty Bean grew restless. Suddenly, she opened her eyes, as she gazed at her Grandmas' antique clock. It was a few minutes past midnight.

Chapter Five

The Black Out

Shorty Bean liked to sleep with the fan on at night. When the fan blades suddenly stopped spinning, it woke her up. She looked over at Smarty, but he was still sleeping peacefully. It was still dark outside. She grabbed her robe and wrapped it around her tightly. Brrrr. It was cold. Then she remembered her father had mentioned that there was a winter storm warning for the area. It was pitch black and before she left her bedroom she heard Grandpa Andy say, "I am working on it. We seem to have lost power," he exclaimed. "I will be up in a bit to check on you, don't worry," he yelled

"Ok, Grandpa" she replied. The conversation woke Smarty. His tail was pointed straight up into the air as he sniffed around to make sure all was safe. And just as Smarty was on guard, Norm's antennas were raised through his fur.

A few minutes passed when she heard Grandpa Andy's footsteps coming up the stairs. She walked quietly down the hallway to meet him. The light from the candle Grandpa Andy held illuminated the pictures of the wall casting an eerie glow and Smarty began to cast shadow puppets taking advantage of the low lighting predicament.

Grandpa Andy walked over to them, "It must be the incoming storm. There was nothing wrong with the fuses. Don't be scared about the power. It will come back on soon. Sometimes a heavy snow places too much weight on the electrical wires and causes them to break. But hopefully the power will be back on by morning," he reassured her.

Once Grandpa Andy had tucked Shorty snuggly back into bed he sat on the edge to talk with Shorty Bean. It was nice to talk about simple things and Shorty laughed as her grandfather told her of a funny story about her dad when he was growing up. As they talked, neither noticed Smarty sneak out of the bedroom and down the stairs. He was on a secret mission.

Shorty loved listening to her grandfather's voice and realized again how much she enjoyed spending time with her grandparents. As they talked, Grandma Ellie pushed open Shorty's bedroom door. "I thought you might need some extra wool blankets to cuddle up with since the electricity is out," she said as she spread a blanket over the top of the bed. As Grandpa Andy moved to give Shorty Bean a kiss, he realized Smarty wasn't there.

"Where's Smarty, do you think he is hiding under the bed?" Grandpa asked. He knelt to look and sneezed. "The only thing under this bed is giant dust balls," he said with another sneeze and a cough. "I will check the kitchen, maybe he became thirsty." Grandpa proceeded to the kitchen. The glow of the lanterns was dim since only a couple were on. He looked around and became distracted as he checked the windows and doors to make sure the house was secured. He completely forgot about Smarty and with a big yawn, headed back for bed.

Shorty Bean anxiously awaited Grandpa Andy's return. But minutes passed and the house had grown silent. She wondered where Smarty could be at this hour of the night.

Chapter Six

Mrs. Patty's Kids

The moon shimmered like snowflakes cascading from the sky. Shorty Bean gazed out her bedroom window and admired the wintry landscape. To her surprise, she saw a pathway of pickling jars glistening in the snow. She had seen something similar this summer as well. Fireflies? she reflected. And if so, how could they be alive this time of the year? As Shorty contemplated the row of jars, she noticed a shadow in the snow along with a red cape blowing in the wind.

Smarty! Shorty Bean grabbed her jacket and backpack and searched her closet for her checkered wool scarf to wrap around her neck. She reached for her heart locket that she had put on the bedside table, but it was not there! How could the locket have vanished? Shorty Bean snatched the candle box and using the shimmering light began to search for the locket. Maybe by chance it had fallen off the bedside table. Or perhaps it could be underneath the bed. But no, she searched both places only to come up empty handed. Perplexed, she gave up the search and tiptoed down the stairs. The worn-out floors were creaky, and the slightest wrong move could wake her grandparents and get her caught!

She breathed a sigh of relief as her foot touched the bottom stair. She moved swiftly to the back door and exited the cottage. But a gust of wind caught the screen door causing it to slam. It woke up Mrs. Patty.

The loud bang from the door made Mrs. Patty's hair stand up on her neck. Instinctively she instructed, "Get inside!"

Shorty Bean heard a loud "BUMP, BUMP" and realized blind Mrs. Patty must have bumped into something from underneath the deck. Shorty Bean jumped off the porch and peered underneath. As her eyes adjusted she saw Mrs. Patty. From underneath her dress, popped out two teeny heads that Shorty Bean did not recognize.

"Well, what do we have here?" Shorty Bean inquired of the two small fur balls Mrs. Patty was protecting. "What are your names?" she asked.

"My name is Kimberly," said the female purring.

"My name is James. We're visiting our Grandma," the other kitten exclaimed.

Kimberly and James had come to stay with Mrs. Patty for the winter season. Kimberly had spotted fur with dazzling ice blue eyes. Her brother, James had black fur with white stripes throughout and blue-green eyes. Both kittens had paws that resembled tiny boots.

"Well, Shorty Bean, you gave me a scare! So those were your little feet creeping down the stairs that I heard? Aren't you up kind of late? Where are you off to on this lovely winter's night?" Mrs. Patty inquired.

"It's Smarty. He has taken off down the garden path," Shorty Bean explained. "I saw his cape and also his paw prints in the snow. I have to talk to him,"

"Oh dear, the secret path is covered with snow. He'll freeze," Mrs. Patty blurted out.

"Oh no! What am I going to do?" Shorty Bean asked.

Mrs. Patty was unique and so was the way she expressed herself. Sometimes it was hard to even understand what she way saying, but Shorty Bean looked past it. She found her comments humorous even though they were completely random.

"Is that what this gorgeous cat heard a while ago, a scatter and a swoosh?" Mrs. Patty stuttered. "That sneaky Smarty! Rats these days, you just can't trust them." Mrs. Patty gave Smarty a rough time, but that was just because she wanted her catkids to hear some much needed wisdom. Being a young cat poses challenges of its own and Mrs. Patty was training them to be watchful of other animals. Smarty was trustworthy, but they would have to find that out on their own.   Even though Mrs. Patty started laughing, Shorty Bean was genuinely worried. She looked off into the distance. "I wonder where Smarty could be? It's cold out there, and I must find him," Shorty Bean said determined to find him! She wrapped the neck scarf more firmly around her neck and zipped up her coat for warmth. She was willing to brave the cold and to do whatever it took to find Smarty!

Chapter Seven

A New Game in Town

"Hey, wait a minute, I have an idea," Mrs. Patty blurted out. Shorty turned around to listen. She could use a good idea right now. She had no idea how to find Smarty.

"A new family of hawks just moved into the oak tree this summer. Maybe they know where he is. I know that Jackie, the leader of the hawks, runs a bingo game on Monday's and the red tree squirrels are always in attendance," Mrs. Patty said. "They might know something," she said with a tip of her hat!

"Do you think they will help?" Shorty Bean asked

"Those red tree squirrels are quick, interesting, jittery, and lack intelligence. I try to confuse them whenever I can," Mrs. Patty began to bang her cane on the deck as she let out a purring laugh. "I mean what else is a gorgeous cat like me to do?" Occasionally Mrs. Patty liked to stir the pot. She was a feisty cat with a quirky sense of humor. "You should go now before it gets any later, but please be careful."

Smarty just listened. He was glad Mrs. Patty wasn't picking on him.

"I will be fine. And I will be careful," Shorty Bean replied as she started to go. "And goodnight Kimberly and James. It was nice to meet you," Shorty said with a wave.

"Goodbye, Shorty Bean. It was great to meet you too," the kittens said. The cat kids leaned into Mrs. Patty rubbing their bodies against her for warmth.

Shorty hadn't gone far when the wind picked up. "I have a bad feeling about this," she thought to herself as she pushed forward to the old oak tree and the bingo game.

As Shorty neared the tree, Jackie the leader of the hawks swooped down and landed right in front, "Do you want me to bring Smarty to you?" said Jackie. "I overheard you talking to Mrs. Patty as I was flying by just now."

"Would you? I would be ever so grateful for your help," Shorty Bean responded.

"I can spot him from the air," Jackie replied it shouldn't take long, she said as she extended her wings and rose into the sky.

Shorty Bean waved as she watched Jackie scan the area. Although she was willing to brave the cold by herself, it was nice to have help. Jackie flew above the trees her sharp eyes watching for any movement. It didn't take long before she caught sight of Smarty's red cape against the white backdrop as he scurried through the snow. Jackie dove straight down to where Smarty was and grabbed him by his cape. With him firmly in her grasp, she turned back toward the oak tree where she had left Shorty.

"Hey, you let me go, or I'll--!" Smarty sputtered as he squirmed in Jackie's grasp.

"You'll what, Smarty?" Jackie asked as she opened her claws and dropped Smarty into a tall pile of snow.

"Helppppp!" Smarty screamed before he plopped into the crusted pile of snow and disappeared. But within seconds his head popped up through the snow. "Brrrr!" He shuddered as he tried to move his whiskers which had frozen solid. He shook his head which sent snow flying and he pulled himself up and out of the pile. He shook his paw in the air at Jackie as he muttered, "I will get you for this. Just you wait and see, Jackieeeeee!"

Jackie landed on one of the lower branches of the oak tree as she let out a mock evil laugh, "Bah, ha, ha, ha, ha!" she finished as she mischievously rubbed her claws together.

Norm the tick rustled the hair on Smarty's back, "Wow, that was some ride," he thought to himself. Good thing he was in tight and wouldn't blow off.

Shorty Bean scooped Smarty up in her arms and gave him a huge hug. "You had me so worried. Why did you leave? And why didn't you answer me? Didn't you hear me calling you?" Shorty Bean scolded.

"Shorty, I have done something awful," Smarty began unable to look her in the eyes. "I took your heart locket off the table. I wanted to find the Coin of Fire for you and so decided to search. I was hoping that the locket would illuminate the dark path and that the map would appear and lead me to the coin." Smarty explained. "I'm so sorry. I must have lost the locket along the path somewhere."

"Smarty, how could you?" Shorty questioned as she processed what the loss of the locket would mean. How could they get it back? Smarty placed his paws over his head in utter shame. "We need to go back to the secret path and follow your footprints before they disappear," Shorty decided. "Hopefully we can find it if we retrace your footsteps."

Smarty was not crazy about searching for the locket in the snow. His paws were already frozen. "I want to go back to the cottage. I'm cold," he complained as Shorty stood with her arms crossed. It was true that the snow was very deep, and the temperatures were plummeting as the wind increased, but Shorty was determined. She wasn't a quitter!

"Smarty, you are the one that got us into this mess. It's your responsibility to help me find it and get us out of this. Suddenly, the north winds began to howl as an enormous gush of snow fell.

Just then, Shorty Bean heard a low whisper which seemed to wind its way through the trees, "Seek, and you will find." Immediately, the sun appeared in all its magnificence. For a moment, Shorty could see the Gazman Forest in a vision. It was so real, it was just like being there. Ben Jeer the King stood before her as he did the past summer when they were searching for all of the Enchanted Coins.

The wintery weather and snow had disappeared and now they stood in a field of green grass and wildflowers. Lady slipper flowers adorned the Thunder Rail Lake and playing music like trumpets. Shorty and Smarty's cold bodies were warmed by summerlike breeze as they

watched the blue birds flutter across the sky as they danced in rhythm with the Lady Slippers tune. It filled them with an instantaneous feeling of hope.

From the corner of her eye, Shorty saw something sparkling. She turned her head just in time to see the locket descend upon the rays of the sun. It swirled over her head and gently came to rest upon her neck.

Shorty Bean turned to Smarty, "I knew the locket couldn't stay lost for long!" she exclaimed as she reached up to touch it. Certain it was securely in place she closed her eyes and took in a deep breath. She smiled as she remembered, the scrolled letter that had mysteriously appeared with the locket describing the power it could release when she released her faith. The scroll was for her eyes only. She still had no idea how or why she had been chosen, but she was grateful.

At that moment, deep within her heart, came the sense that she needed to see White Cloud, the bald eagle who was the ruler of the Gazman Forest. He had been her protector and it felt safe in his presence. Yet even as she thought of him, the dark forces who sought the locket's power crept in and tried to steal her hope.

As she contemplated what to do, the sun suddenly disappeared. The sunny day turned dark as menacing clouds rolled in. Shorty wasn't afraid. She knew the way home. She closed her eyes and believed remembering what the letter said the first time she discovered the locket. As she kept her mind focused, faith increased inside her and in no time at all she found herself back at the cottage standing in the snow with Smarty beside her.

Chapter Eight

Chores out Back

Shorty Bean held the locket tightly. She realized the three coins of the dove, the heart, and the wind were now secure; yet she could not help but think back on how the fourth coin, the Coin of Fire, which had fallen from her hands the summer before. A buzzing noise grew louder and louder. Shorty understood what that meant. The electrical power had returned to the cottage. As the electricity flowed through the electrical lines, suddenly the dark cottage lit the way from them like a beacon of light.

"Smarty we have to get back before everyone wakes up and discovers we've been missing. Let's go!" The two turned ran back to the cottage, but not before they engaged in a rather ridiculous and spontaneous snow ball fight. After all snowball fights are quite fun. Smarty formed a tiny snow ball with his paws and whipped the pellet directly into Shorty Bean's hair.

"Okay, you've had it," Shorty Bean pointed her finger at him as she tried to act angry, but started to laugh. "I'm going to get you!"

Smarty smirked, "What did I do? It wasn't me!"

In response, Shorty Bean formed several large snow balls and fired them at Smarty as he hopped back and forth trying to avoid getting hit. Swish. Swish. Two zipped past him missing him by inches. Ha! He had escaped. He started to laugh when WAP, right in the googles!

Once they stepped inside the cottage they tiptoed and hurried up the stairs. Quickly but quietly they pulled off their hats, gloves and coats and started to crawl into bed when Grandpa peeked his head in and said, "I'm glad you found Smarty!"

"Me, too. Thanks, Grandpa! Goodnight," she said softly.

"Goodnight, honey. Sleep well," he said as he pulled the comforter up over her shoulders. Both Shorty and Smarty were asleep before he ever left the room.

The sun was streaming through the sheer curtains the next morning waking Shorty from her short night's rest. She did not want to get out of bed. Neither did Smarty. He pulled the covers over both of their heads and snuggled back into his pillow next to Shorty.

But the next moment the covers were being yanked off and the cold air hit his body sending shivers down his spine.

"What are you doing?" he asked grumpily. But before Shorty could reply, the smell of bacon and eggs filled the air. They both looked at each other.

"Breakfast, now that is what I am talking about!" they both said simultaneously. In a flash they both hopped out of bed and were racing downstairs to the breakfast table.

"How did you sleep last night?" Grandpa Andy asked with a wink. Shorty Bean had a sneaky suspicion he knew something, but if he wasn't going to say anything, then neither would she.

"Great, even though Smarty kept me up all night snorting!" Shorty replied.

"Snorting? You mean snoring?" he corrected. She really meant snorting because he sounded just like a pig when he snored.

Shorty Bean chuckled as her Dad raised his finger pointing at Smarty, "I told you to get rid of that rat!"

"Don't say that, she loves that creature." Mom said.

"Creature? Okay, whatever you want to call him," Dad stated as he rolled his eyes.

"Can you pass the bacon?" Shorty Bean asked sweetly as she sat down to eat. As her mother passed the heaping platter to her, she pulled off three thick slices. Yum! When she thought no one was watching she slid one of the pieces into her hand, broke it in half and then under the table to feed Smarty. Bacon was his favorite! Smarty took it gently from her hand. As he did, a small corner broke off and landed on the back of his fur.

Norm the tick wiggled over for a quick bite. "Yum, that's delicious!" Norm was no ordinary tick after all ticks don't normally eat bacon, but this one sure did!Smarty continued to make begging noises for more bacon. When he was around adults he lost his table manners. As soon as they finished eating Shorty Bean volunteered to shovel the snow off the sidewalk. She did want Smarty to get in trouble. "Check in the shed for the snow shovel," Grandpa Andy instructed her.

"Ok, thanks Grandpa," she replied as she turned to Smarty, "Come on, boy, we'll get right on that!"

As the two made their way through the snow to the shed, Shorty opened the side door. It was dark inside. She peered into the inky blackness until her eyes adjusted and she could find the shovel with the wooden handle. Shaking the snow off his paws, Smarty crept in behind her. Just as Shorty Bean turned to head back outside, the door slammed shut. Now it was completely black inside. Smarty began to shake, and Shorty's heart was pounding so fast it seemed it would come out of her chest. "It's ok, Smarty," Shorty comforted him. "It's just the wind," she said as she felt along the wall for the door. Then the ground broke open and they both began to slide down a long, dark tunnel.

Chapter Nine

The Secret
Passageway

The locket encircling Shorty's neck began to glow as they slid down the chute. They came to a sudden stop. Shorty stood. "Are you ok, Smarty? Are you hurt?"

"That was AWESOME!" he shouted. "Let's do it again!"

"There's not time for that, Smarty. We have to see where this leads!" Shorty instructed.

The glow from the locket cast a small light into the darkness. "Where are we?" Shorty asked Smarty, not that she expected him to know. As she looked down she could see they were standing on a ledge.

"Smarty, we have to get down there," Shorty informed him as she noticed a plateau with a ladder leading into a tunnel. Smarty inhaled deeply. As he did, he blew up like a puffer fish.

"Smarty, you're brilliant!" Shorty Bean declared as she grabbed the four corners of his cape. Clutching them tightly in both hands she waited until they filled with air like a parachute. "One, two three. Here we go!" Shorty shouted as she held tightly to the cape and they glided gently down to the next level.

When Shorty's toe hit the ground, she couldn't get her balance. Down they both went and rolled to a stop. When the dust finally cleared, Shorty stood and tested her ankles. Both she and Smarty were both fine. She dusted the dirt from her legs and peered around.

Smarty took his paws and pressed in his cheeks to let the excess air out. For a moment they hung down like a couple of sagging balloons, but after a couple of shakes of his head back and forth, they went back to normal.

"Where are we?" Smarty asked.

"It appears to be an underground pathway," Shorty responded.

"Where are we?" Norm mimicked Smarty only this time he was later responding. The signal from Norm's antennas clearly was not working properly.

Confused Shorty responded, "I already told you. Weren't you listening?" The light from her locket began to glow even stronger, penetrating the darkness and providing guidance as they inched their way along the path.

There were tangled roots growing across the winding pathway as they delicately picked their way through the path. "It looks like a small ladder," Shorty almost shouted. Not one to hesitate when an adventure revealed itself, Shorty Bean climbed the first rung and Smarty followed.

"Are you sure about this?" Smarty asked as they continued up the ladder rung by rung.

"No, I'm not sure! But what have we got to lose. Come on!" Shorty shouted down to him. As they continued to climb the latter, it took them to an opening and out to what was a familiar place. Shorty realized they were at Ms. Nora's tree home! They had discovered it after receiving directions from a purple rose in the garden last summer. As they climbed out of the tunnel it startled Ms. Nora.

"Shiver me timbers darling. Yaw about scared me half to death." Ms. Nora declared breathing heavily as she held her paw on her chest. "Now, the both of you, come and sit and have some tea," she invited.

Shorty Bean and Smarty accepted her kind invitation and sat down as Ms. Nora rushed inside to pour them each some tea and grab some tiny cakes. She quickly returned with a platter brimming with three cups of steaming liquid. The locket around Shorty Bean's neck began to shine. Ms. Nora, always the perfect host, noticed it, but she didn't say anything.

"Thank you, Ms. Nora," Shorty said as she took a sip of tea.

"Yuck, this is not tea! What is it?" Smarty sputtered as he spit out the hot liquid.

"It's not tea? And nobody knows it but me." Ms. Nora danced a jig as she sang her rhyme circling around her wooden table.

"No really, what kind of drink is it?" Shorty inquired.

"Why that's green tree bark sap," Ms. Nora replied. "Only the best for my guests," she declared as she took a big sip.

Neither Shorty or Smarty cared too much for the taste of the strange drink, but politely ate the cakes and did their best to take several sips. Truth be told, Ms. Nora's tea was an acquired taste.

"How did you happen upon me secret path in the roots of Nussle Ridge Creek?" Ms. Nora questioned.

"Well, we found it by accident, as we were doing a chore for my Grandpa Andy. We were out back in the shed to get a shovel when suddenly the ground broke open and we started to fall. Eventually the dark tunnel led us here to you," Shorty finished.

"The pathway is a secret that hasn't been used for many years," Ms. Nora explained. "No one must know about it. You must be careful not to utter a word because there are spies in the forest."

Shorty Bean understood her meaning and knew she had to be careful. Foes lurked in the forest such as the black bears, the black ravens and the northern winds. Shorty Bean and Smarty promised not to say anything to anyone.

"Thank you. Then let's seal it with a jig!" Ms. Nora began to sing. "Dance with glee with a cup of tea, for an Irish jig, I say, I say for an Irish jig, I say." When they stopped dancing, Shorty Bean realized if she waited much longer, her grandparents may get worried of her time outside doing her chores with Smarty. "You can't leave empty-handed," Ms. Nora declared as she packed some cabbage and beef in a tiny wooden container and wrapped it in muslin fabric.

Smarty and Shorty Bean thanked her for the hospitality as they got up to leave her home. It was then that Shorty remembered that they needed to find White Cloud. She wondered what had happened to his nest since the last time they had met. In the vision it was empty. She wondered why he had he abandoned it and if he would ever return.

"Ms. Nora, it's hard for me sometimes. I desire to have faith, but my mind gets crowded with so many negative thoughts," Shorty said in a small voice.

"Pay no attention to those thoughts you be hearin'. They're evil," Ms. Nora encouraged her. "Always remember your locket and faith will keep you strong and safe. Faith will guide you, just believe."

The two embraced as Shorty and Smarty prepared to leave. She desperately wanted to believe that, but in reality could she?

Chapter Ten

Ice Fishing Bubbles

The weather conditions were getting worse. Shorty Bean pulled the collar of her coat tighter around her neck to shield her from the biting north winds. She shivered uncontrollably but remained on the path trudging through the deepening snow. Her cheeks burned, and her nose tingled.

"Smarty we have to find shelter," Shorty declared as she felt his tiny body shivering as uncontrollably as her own. She opened the locket which displayed the golden coins of power and closed her eyes. "I believe," she spoke into the swirling wind as it took her words and tossed them into the sky. But even as they disappeared a virtual landscape of the Dix River appeared before her. She saw the dense wooded trees and watched as the water flowed before her but in an instant, the scenery changed and they were back in the snow once again. The vision from the locket gave her hope. Instantly she knew what she needed to do. "I don't know what happened, Smarty," Shorty told him as she hugged him close. "I tried to believe, but it's hard to have faith in what you can't see sometimes. But I know what to do. Grandpa Andy taught me. Let's gather some sticks," she said with confidence ready to put her plan in motion.

"First, we need to start a fire to get warm and then I will see if I can catch a fish for us my friend," she said in an attempt to cheer him up. "Grandpa Andy taught me how to ice fish a couple of years ago. You'll see. It's fun!"

"But I'm freezing!" Smarty exclaimed

"Smarty, find a branch so I can make a fishing pole," she instructed.

Smarty found a large twig and tried to carry it in his mouth to Shorty. However, the weight was not proportioned, and he fell over on his side. At first Shorty Bean thought he was playing, but then realized that he was having trouble carrying it and needed help. She picked up the stick and dusted the snow off Smarty's face. He was relieved.

Together they gathered long pine tree branches that had fallen to the ground. Shorty stacked them in the fashion of a teepee so that they had some shelter from the harsh wind.

"Now what can we do for a fire?" she mused as Smarty dropped a bundle of twigs in front of her. "Oh Smarty, these are perfect for kindling the fire. Well done! Now to get it started..." Shorty Bean located two small sand pebbles and began to click them together the way her grandfather had taught her. The grainy sand consistency imbedded in the rock caused it to spark as she struck them together. After several attempts a spark ignited the pine needles. Excited, Shorty Bean blew gently as Smarty stood by ready to add more needles to coax it into a flame. But just as quickly as it started, the fire disappeared as the northern winds gusted past their shelter putting out the tiny flame.

"How will we ever keep this going?" Shorty Bean hung her head in frustration ready to give up. She had to really be tired as it wasn't in her nature to just walk away from a challenge. She grasped hold of the locket around her neck.

The locket began to illuminate, and the sun shone brightly dispersing the clouds. "I have an idea!" Smarty said as he removed his goggles. Using the goggle lens, he raised them towards the sun's rays. A beam of sunlight radiated through the lens until a small flame sparked. They coaxed it into a larger flame as they slowly added more kindling and finally some larger logs. Shorty Bean high fived Smarty. Just having a little light and heat did much to chase away the discouragement that had descended upon them and lifted their spirits.

Shorty sat in front of the fire and began to rub her hands together to get the circulation going again. She and Smarty started to warm up as they stood near the billowing clouds of steam arose from the fire.

"What's going on?" Smarty wondered as the hiss of the steam increased. In an instant, the fire disappeared.

Once the smoke cleared, Shorty understood. "Perfect!" she exclaimed "The fire melted a hole in the ice for us. Now I can try to catch us a fish," Shorty explained as she yanked out a strand of her hair attached it to a stick and tied a safety pin that had been attached to her coat on for a hook. Within a few seconds she had a homemade fishing pole.

Shorty Bean and Smarty stared into the dark water when a strange fish appeared. "Smarty, do you think it's Sir. Davy?" Shorty asked. They had met Sir Davy on one of their adventures last summer when Shorty had caught him fishing. But she soon learned that Sir Davy wasn't in the mood to be eaten.

"Look, down in the hole at the bubbles!" Shorty said as he pointed to the water.

They could hear a muffled voice, but not clear enough to understand.

"Smarty, did you hear what was said?" Shorty Bean asked him.

"Don't ask me, I hear voices," he said only half joking. "But no, I couldn't figure it out."

"Don't ask me, I hear voices," Norm mimicked.

"Wise guy," Smarty replied.

Shorty Bean chuckled. She enjoyed their playful exchange. Just then a familiar face peeked up at her from the water. "It's you, it's you, Sir Davy, it's you!" she exclaimed clapping her hands as the fishing pole clattered to the ice. The freshwater fish jumped out of the water and saluted them with his fin.

"Greetings, Shorty Bean. I say attention and welcome back," Sir Davy said.

"Sir Davy, we've come to the river to find White Cloud," Shorty informed him. "Do you know where we can find him?"

"Well, that could be a problem," Sir Davy replied. "After you and Smarty left last summer, the lake began to freeze. The north winds had evidently followed you to us. I can't remember the last time it has been so cold, and our river hadn't frozen for years. The unrelenting wind forced White Cloud to abandon his tree nest, but we all still feel his presence."

"So, no one knows where he went?" Shorty asked.

"White Cloud told everyone in the forest that he was leaving to go to the place of light," Sir Davy responded.

Shorty Bean wondered where the place of light was located and how she might find it. "So where is it from here? Is it far?" she inquired.

I have never been there, but there is a place of light high above the clouds where I believe White Cloud now lives, Sir Davy finished as he jumped back into the water. He raised his fin into the air to wave goodbye to Shorty Bean as he swam away.

"But I have more questions," she cried out. But Sir Davy had already disappeared into the dark swirling water. Just as quickly as he appeared, he had disappeared leaving behind a flurry of bubbles in his trail. As they rose to the surface they popped one by one.

"It's a message!" Shorty cried out as she listened closely, as the bubbles popped.

"Seek."

"And."

"You."

"Will."

"Find."

After the last bubble had popped, Shorty smiled. Although Sir Davy had left, they were not alone. She could sense White Cloud's presence just as Sir Davy had said.

Soon the Gazman Forest was alight with tiny lights glistening from every tree. It provided just enough light to enable her to see the path. She could see footprints in the snow and decided to follow them. After several turns, they disappeared right in front of a huge towering pine.

Shorty Bean tilted her head to look into the branches. She could hear wrestling among the branches overhead but couldn't see anything in the darkness.

Now what?

Chapter Eleven

Keep Out!

As they stood at the base of the tree, Shorty sensed danger. She looked up and saw in the large oak tree an orange arrow pointed right at her. It was Tripod, the box turtle. He was agile for a box turtle. He had strong claws which helped him to climb with ease, a hard shell that helped protect him from pointy branches and a mechanical leg. It was useful to allow him to brace against the trunk and provided just the right balance to prevent a nasty tumble. Obviously, he was not your typical turtle and he was the Defender of the Gazman Forest. They had met him last summer.

"Don't move or I'll shoot this arrow," he threatened. He held the bow unwaveringly. Norm's antennas went berserk as the tension built.

"Tripod, it is me, Shorty Bean, and Smarty. Remember us? And how did you get so high up in the tree if you don't mind my asking?' Shorty continued. You're a turtle! And yet Tripod was fierce and not someone you wanted to mess with. He was made the defender of the forest for a reason and he was not afraid to defend anything.

Tripod looked down at Smarty's fur as he said, "I remember you! But what is that on your back? It looks like an antenna!" Tripod now aimed the arrow at Smarty.

Norm flattened his body down like a pancake into Smarty's fur.

"Tripod you need to calm down, I think you're seeing things again," Smarty said

Norm started to mimic Smarty when Tripod intercepted and called out, "Looks like there is a spy in our midst and he's hiding in your…" Just then a large shadow crept over them and the north winds began to howl. Distracted, Tripod turned his attention to the shadow. Once the darkness lifted, Shorty inquired of him.

"We are looking for White Cloud. Do you know where he is?" Shorty and Smarty looked at each other, but said nothing. It was obvious they thought Tripod was losing his mind. Tripod didn't say anything. He still glared at Smarty's fur. Smarty waged his tail in hopes to distract him.

"Smarty, I'm not a spy, trust me!" Norm pleaded.

Tripod examined Smarty's fur, but could not see anything. Shorty Bean and Smarty looked at each other with wide eyes. What did he think he was going to find?

Without warning Tripod lowered the bow, satisfied at least for the moment that they were safe. "Well, well. What are you doing here in the forest, this time of year?" he asked them. Shorty Bean felt confused. It was like Tripod was seeing them for the first time. She was just about to inquire further when suddenly Smarty screamed.

"Quick, get down on the ground. The black bears are coming!" Smarty scurried up on Tripod's shoulders as his knees shook uncontrollably.

Tripod, rolled his eyes as he watched the bears approach. He could handle them.

"That must have been the shadow that came over us a moment ago," Shorty said. "It was a warning and we missed it."

"You can't fight them alone. I, Tripod, The Defender of the Box Turtles stand with you," he declared bravely with his arm upraised. He bowed his head for a moment as he rotated his mechanical leg. In the next moment he jumped to the ground. "SHHHHH, be quiet! Spies. Choppers! Get down on the ground and don't move!" he instructed.

Tripod was certain there were spies. And there were, but not what he expected. It was the Black Bears seeking the power of the locket. Tripod planted his feet and raised his bow. That was not going to happen when he was around.

Shorty and Smarty watched as Tripod became more unpredictable by the moment. He was engaged and ready to defend them and the forest. His eyes darted back and forth almost frantically as he scouted the area. The roar of the bears grew distant. Shorty and Smarty both let out deep breaths. They were safe at least for now.

"We need to find White Cloud," Shorty insisted unwilling to give up the search. "Do you know where he is?" she asked.

"How long have you been out here?" Tripod asked. "Your teeth are chattering! You cannot continue to search for White Cloud until you get warmed up. Come back to my home with me and I will serve you some of my famous vegetable soup. It's been simmering all day."

Norm wisely remained as flat as a pancake. He knew better than to mimic Smarty or move with Tripod around.

Tripod took the lead and within a few minutes they arrived at his hut. He opened the door and held it open for them. As they entered they were met with a delicious smell coming from a black kettle that was bubbling over the fire. Shorty's stomach growled.

"Have a seat and let me get you some food. Tripod quickly ladled a generous portion into two bowls. "Ah, here you go," he said as he placed the steaming soup in front of Shorty. "And here's a small cup for you as well, my friend," he said as he placed Smarty's meal on the floor. Smarty began to snort. Normally he only did this when he was sleeping, but he was so excited for some food it just came out!

"I'll just be over here, by my lonesome, practically starving, don't worry about me," whispered Norm as he rubbed his antennas together like he was playing a miniature violin. Smarty ignored him. He was more interested in food than self-pity.

"Mmmmm. This is delicious," Shorty commented as the hot liquid filled her stomach and warmed her body. This was just what they needed to help them keep going. Shorty Bean then remembered the special package Ms. Nora made for her and Smarty. She unraveled the muslin and gave both Smarty and Tripod a small piece of beef. It went perfect with the meal and they were very grateful!

While they were eating, Tripod had an idea of a way to get the red tree squirrels back. They often caused havoc in the trees, which Tripod liked to climb. He had a personal vendetta against them and thought of something that might just get them back, Tripod style! He had explosives along with many beakers in his home. He enjoyed watching things explode.

"Tripod listen, my friend. I need a favor," Smarty said as he while placed his paw on Tripod's shell.

"What would that be," Tripod asked. He raised an eyebrow and sat silently until Smarty continued. He was curious what the little creature had to say.

"Jackie the Hawk has some red tree squirrels. They need to have some special nuts to help them when they play bingo, if you know what I am saying?" Smarty said with a wink.

Tripod grinned. He knew exactly what Smarty meant.

"So, my friend, do you think you can help me out?" Smarty asked.

"I can indeed," he said as he reached over into his cabinet and pulled out a velvet bag. Tripod opened it. Walnuts flew over the table. Smarty's eyes opened wide. He was tempted to eat one. He reached out to grab one when Tripod stopped him.

"No, don't eat any of these," he insisted as he put his hand over Smarty's. These are no ordinary walnuts," he began. "They are infused with gun powder. When they cracked open they will explode like a firecracker. They are for your furry friends," Tripod explained as he scooped the walnuts back into the velvet bag and handed it to Smarty. "They will help the squirrels, let's just say, be a little more interesting this next game," as Tripod laughed as he winked at Smarty.

Smarty nodded and smiled his thanks as he took the bag from Tripod and placed it in one of the adventure patches on his red cape.

"Can you take us to see White Cloud now," Shorty Bean asked now that they had finished their meal.

"Of course, I can. But we will have to wait until morning. It's cold and dark now and unsafe to travel the paths at night. The Black Bears may be out patrolling the area again. Get a good night's sleep and we will start off first thing in the morning when the bears are asleep."

Shorty slept peacefully in a potato bed covered with celery leaves. Shorty couldn't stretch out completely, but was surprised how comfortable the bed felt. Smarty decided the bed was only big enough for one and chose to curl up in the backpack with his head hanging out the side. Before too long his nose began to sniff the celery and CHOMP, he took a bite of the bed. If you have been around anyone eating celery before, you know it can be extremely loud. The sound from his chomping disturbed Norm.

With antennae jerking wildly, Norm expanded puffing up almost three times in size. Annoyed, he stomped his eight legs to aggravate Smarty and make him stop chomping. It worked! Smarty leaned in to itch his back with his hind legs, but he felt no relief as Norm kept moving to avoid detection.

Norm's antennas continued to jerk and making an irritating screeching sound. "Smarty, knock it off," Shorty insisted as she rolled over on her back.

Smarty closed his mouth and continued to chew the celery only quieter now. As he chewed, a nut from the patch on his cape escaped and fell to the ground. It rolled into the corner coming to a stop as it hit the baseboard.

Smarty stopped chewing. He could hear someone else munching in the darkness. Unbeknown to him, it was a tiny mouse. There was a small explosion and a burst of light. The tiny mouse launched into the air, as sparks flew. It was like the fourth of July! Laughing until his sides hurt, Smarty reflected on how the nuts would affect the red tree squirrels and their leader Jackie. He looked over at Shorty Bean and realized she had missed the whole thing. She was fast asleep. Whew that was a close one!" he thought to himself.

Smarty imagined how the walnuts would work on the red tree squirrels. In his mind he envisioned them in a frenzy, bouncing through the limbs of the oak tree near the cottage. He dodged as they flew launching over his head. Mrs. Patty was right. Those squirrels were rather crazy! Smarty spent the rest of the night dodging squirrels and shooting acorns at them from his slingshot. By the time the sun rose, and rays of light began to peek through the window, Shorty rose well rested. Smarty, on the other hand, was exhausted.

"Smarty what's the matter?" Shorty asked. "You look tired."

"Well how could I be otherwise," he commented grouchily. "I spent all night saving you and dodging the squirrels."

Shorty and Tripod exchanged a humorous look, and both started to laugh. They realized that Smarty had been dreaming!

"Thank you for your kindness," Shorty said as she pulled on her coat and hat. "How long will it take us to get to White Cloud's new nest?" she asked.

"We should get there before noon if we leave now. It's quite a journey, but I will help you," Tripod said as he grabbed his trusty bow and quiver of arrows. The threesome trudged along in silence down the snowy path in search of White Cloud. The northern winds seemed to sense the presence of the travelers and blew heavily against them. It took all of Shorty's energy to press into the wind and keep on going.

"Smarty, stay inside and try to keep warm," she instructed as she made sure her backpack was zipped only partly closed so he could breathe. At least he could get out of the wind. As the sun rose higher in the sky, in the distance they heard a loud roar.

"We must hurry," Tripod stated firmly. "The Black Bears are awake and will see our trail. They will do whatever it takes to prevent us from reaching White Cloud."

Sure, enough as the travelers quickened their pace they saw a swarm of black ravens against the pale sky descending toward them.

"Keep your head down and wave your arms over your head. As long as we keep moving they should not be able to harm us. I think White Cloud's nest is just over that hill."

Tripod was right about two things, but as they were soon to find out, he was very wrong about the third.

The black ravens although annoying, made no attempt to harm them as long as they kept moving. And Tripod was correct. White Cloud's nest was just over the next hill. The only problem was White Cloud wasn't. The nest was abandoned.

"What do we do now?" Shorty cried. How were they ever going to find the Coin of Fire if they couldn't locate White Cloud?

"You must go back to your grandparent's cottage. You are too tired to continue this journey and they will be worried about you. You have done well. Let me continue the search to find White Cloud for you. I fear that this will be a dangerous undertaking and I tell you, you must go back!"

Smarty jumped at Tripods tone and insistence and scurried back into the backpack. He peeked out the top as Tripod continued, "I have a special serum that comes from a secret plant. Use it only if absolutely necessary and use it sparingly," he said as he handed Shorty a small brown bottle. "The result of the hot bubbly liquid can be rather explosive, but it will protect you on your return journey since I cannot be with you," Tripod finished. No wonder he had earned the title of Defender. His very nature was trying to protect Shorty and Smarty even when he couldn't be with them.

"Have this handy with you on the rest of your journey," he insisted as he saluted them.

"Don't leave yet," Shorty pleaded with him. "What can the serum do? How do I use it?"

"Well, you could start by reading the instructions," Tripod said with a laugh trying to break the tension. "Drink just one teaspoon and you will be able to run at the speed of light!"

"Ha, then maybe I will take two. Just think what I could do then?" Smarty said with a laugh.

"Enough!" Tripod growled at him completely serious once again. He pointed to the warning label in bright red on the bottle, "Do not drink more than a teaspoon of the serum or you may explode into the air like a rocket!"

"Why, thank you, I think…" Shorty responded as she took the bottle from him. "We will be careful!" Shorty Bean placed the bottle gently in her backpack and waved goodbye as she and Smarty went one way and Tripod went another. She hoped he could find White Cloud soon.

She hoped she could find her way home.

About thirty minutes later, Shorty felt her backpack rumble and then vibrate violently against her back. She jerked it off. "Smarty are you okay?"

BOOM! Smarty catapulted out of the backpack straight into the sky. "HEEEELLLLPPPP MEEEEEEE!"

she heard him squeal as she saw fire and smoke shooting out his feet.

She shook her head as she watched the inevitable for what goes up, must come down as Smarty crashed down landing into a mound of snow.

"It's a good thing there was snow here," Shorty said as she reached down to pull him out. He was covered in grey soot and his hair resembled deep-fried French fries. She raised an eye brow and shook her head again as she said, "Obviously, you drank the serum that Tripod made. Didn't you hear what he said? How it would make you explode, like a rocket?"

Smarty let out a loud burp. "Let's do that again!" he said even as smoke continued to smolder from his feet.

Norm agreed, "Yeah! Let's do that again!"

Shorty Bean burst out laughing as she dusted Smarty off and helped him climb back into the backpack. At least they knew the serum worked! But she trembled at the thought that they very well could need it with what lay ahead.

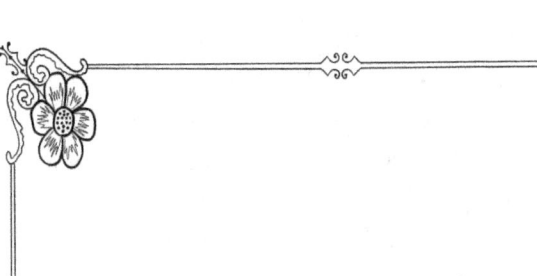

Chapter Twelve

Flicked by Jackie

Shorty and Smarty trudged through the snow for what seemed like hours. But once they reached the pickling jars at the edge of the forest, Shorty knew the cottage was near. She breathed a sigh of relief as the back steps of the porch came into view. Just as her foot hit the first step, however, Jackie the hawk swooped down and snatched Smarty up by his head yanking him out of the backpack.

"HELP!" Smarty screamed.

The hawk ascended higher and higher into the air with Smarty in her grasp when suddenly released him.

"Ah ha haa haa!" Jackie laughed as she swooped toward the ground. She came so close to Shorty that she could see the yellow of her evil eyes.

"Smarty!" Shorty screamed as she watched her friend plummet toward the ground. She was riveted in place unable to move. She knew he couldn't survive such a fall, but seemed powerless to stop it. Just then a red tree squirrel flew from the tree to cushion Smarty's fall. He landed on the ground and spread out like a trampoline just as Smarty landed on him. He hit him dead on.

The squirrel lay still with his eyes bulging out of his head, flattened like a pancake from the impact. Smarty got up and shook his head. He was a little dizzy from the fall and smashing into the squirrel. "Wow, I know that hurt, buddy; I feel your pain," he said as he reached out a paw to the squirrel to help him up. "What on earth caused you to help me?"

"Well, it's not because I like you particularly," the squirrel began. "So don't get the wrong idea. But Shorty's grandma always leaves nuts and bread on the ground for us in the winter, so we will have enough food. I know she likes you and well, I like her. So I decided by saving you, I was actually repaying Grandma Ellie for her kindness.

"Okay, gotcha. Okay well, thank you for saving me. And just so you know, I don't like you much either," he said with a sassy smile. Smarty reached in his cape and pulled out a handful of walnuts. He tossed them into the air for the squirrel who tipped his head in thanks.

"Come on, Smarty, it's time to go inside!" Shorty Bean hollered as scooped him up. "You gave me such a scare," she exclaimed as she looked him over. "Are you hurt?"

"I'm fine! What a rush. That was amazing!" he stated. But actually, his heart was still beating fast from his close call.

"What is that look on your face for?" Shorty asked as she looked at Smarty. "What have you done? I know that look. You're up to something."

Just then the red squirrel, who had been gathering the walnuts and storing them in his mouth began to ping up into the air. He resembled a Mexican jumping bean!

"Smarty! Did you dip those walnuts in that serum?"

Smarty only snickered in response. Next he would have to figure out how to get even with Jackie too! As they entered the cottage all Shorty wanted to do was get something to eat and lay down. Her legs hurt from all the walking they had done the last two days.

"Did you clear a pathway for your Grandpa?" her dad asked as she started to sit down.

"Oops!" Smarty and Shorty glanced at each other and laughed. It was still the exact same time as when the adventure had begun. "Sorry, Dad! We'll get right on it," Shorty been replied as she jumped off the sofa with Smarty in tow.

Later that night after Grandma Ellie tucked them in bed she knelt by the bed as she always did and closed her eyes. She folded her hands and began to pray, "As night falls and the sky begins to sleep, I pray the Lord your soul to keep. I know that angels will be sitting nearby, to watch you at night and fly, fly, fly. Snuggle in bed, my dear, and dream of candy canes and elephant ears. Think about what daybreak will bring, as we wake to another day and sing. Bless the skies, the oceans, the seasons and the sun. Bless mommies and daddies and little girls too, and Smarties and grandpas and grandmas too. And help us to always remember You, You, You. Amen. I love you. Sleep well," she instructed as she bent down to kiss Shorty on the forehead.

"Goodnight, Grandma." Shorty Bean replied as she blew her a kiss. "Night falls and the sky begins to sleep. I pray the Lord your soul to keep. I know that Angels will be sitting nearby, to watch you at night and fly, fly, fly. Tuck yourself in bed my dear, and dream of candies and elephant ears, and think about what daybreak will bring, when we spend the day together and watch the morning shine and sing. God bless us, everyone the skies, the oceans, the seasons, and the sun. Bless Mommies and Daddies and little girls too and Smarties and Grandpas and Grandmas too, and help us to always Remember you, you, you. AMEN."

Grandma Ellie turned the lamp down low, so the room was dark, but Shorty could see just enough if she needed to get up. She let out a contented sigh as Smarty snuggled close to her for warmth. They were both almost asleep when a loud banging noise crashed overhead from the attic.

"Did you hear that, Smarty?" she asked.

"Loud and clear, Shorty Bean. What do you think it was?" he responded. He really didn't want to get out of the warm bed, but Shorty was already up and wrapping her coat around her.

"I don't know, but we are going to find out, "she replied as she grabbed her flashlight and opened the bedroom door.

The two peered around trying to figure out the source of the banging, but the house was silent. They began to wonder if it had really happened, or if it had just been a dream. "Could we be dreaming the same dream?" Shorty asked Smarty with a laugh. She opened the back door just to make sure that all was okay. She and Smarty stepped out onto the porch and down into the yard. The moon was full, and the stars seemed to dance in the sky. They both stared into the sky in awe of the twinkling stars intertwined with the beauty and colors of the night.

"Look at the reddish planet," Shorty said to Smarty as she pointed toward the north. They admired the constellations and the streaks of purple, blue and turquoise streaks that could only be seen at certain times of the year.

Smarty laid down in the snow and started to make a snow angel as he moved his arms and legs up and down and back and forth. Shorty laughed as she watched and then decided to make her own snow angel beside his. When they finished they laughed as they admired their handiwork and to their amazement, the snow angels came to life and flew into the night sky, holding hands and singing.

As they continued to gaze at the sky, there was a bright flash and Shorty Bean could see White Cloud's face. "Seek and you shall find!" she heard him rumble.

She and Smarty looked at each other, but didn't say a word. What was there to say? Together they turned and walked back into the house locking the door and then headed back upstairs to bed.

Exhausted, Shorty and Smarty crawled back into bed and dreamed of snow angels that came to life. Smarty tried to get comfortable, but became aware of a terrible itch on his back. He started to scratch harder and harder.

"Stop it! I'm over here," a small voice insisted.

Smarty ignored it convinced it was his imagination.

"Where does it itch, can I help you?" Shorty asked. She could tell he was in distress.

"Yes, it's driving me nuts!" Smarty declared as he pointed to the itch. Shorty Bean scratched several spots, but couldn't seem to relieve Smarty's discomfort.

"You didn't get it!" he cried.

"You didn't get it!" A small voice mimicked.

"Did you hear that?" Smarty asked. He shook his head. Was he losing it?

"Hear what?" Shorty asked.

"Nothing, don't worry about it," he said as he tried to curl up and go to sleep, but it was like there was a war going on in his fur.

Then Shorty Bean noticed something wrestling back and forth in Smarty's fur. "Don't move," she instructed. But the tone of her voice was enough to set him off.

"What is it? Get it off me; I am going to freak out! Get it off me!" Smarty insisted as he danced about swatting at his back.

"Smarty, I think it is a tick!" Shorty exclaimed.

"Get it off! Please get it off me," Smarty pleaded.

As she moved her fingers through his fur she bumped into the problem. "Do you have a name?" she asked as she separated the fur to see him better.

"Norm. I am Norm the tick," he introduced himself.

"Norm? What are you doing there? At least I'm not going insane," Smarty stated. "I just have a tick on my back named Norm that repeats everything I say. Just put me out of my misery," he declared as he rolled over with exaggerated drama as if he were dead.

Shorty rolled her eyes. "Oh, brother," she exclaimed at Smarty's antics. Well, it looks like Norm will be sticking around for a while," she told him. "I cannot seem to get him off your fur."

Chapter Thirteen

Winter Wonderland

"Shorty Bean, your dad and I were thinking about going into town for the day to do some last minute shopping before Christmas tomorrow and get some pizza. What do you think?"

"That sounds like a great idea!" she said before she stuffed another big bite of biscuits and gravy in her mouth. Pizza was one of her favorite foods and biscuits and gravy was another. So far the day was shaping up pretty well. "Can Smarty come, too?" she asked. "He likes the melted cheese and eats any of the burnt pepperoni." Smarty jumped up and down and nodded his head. He wanted to come, too!

They quickly finished breakfast, cleaned up the dishes and ran to get their coats. It wasn't just the day before Christmas. It was also the day before Shorty Bean's birthday! She couldn't wait.

Needing to get a few last items for their Christmas celebration and for Shorty's birthday celebration, her parents decided to make it a special event. Shorty always loved to go into town at Christmas time for the townspeople created a glorious Christmas display each year that was full of wonder. As they walked the sidewalk and entered the town square there were people passing out homemade peanut butter cookies, paper cups of hot cocoa and chocolate covered apples. It was delicious. Smarty and Shorty Bean loved sampling the local food. Smarty gobbled part of a cookie and then licked his lips. He loved Christmas!

They spent the next hour going in and out of the little shops along the main street. There were lots of last minute shoppers and it felt very festive as the Christmas music from the stores followed them out onto the sidewalk. Shorty saw her mom up ahead of them.

"Boy, Mom. You've had some fun, haven't you?" Shorty commented as she noticed several different purchases her mother had made. Many of the bags held Christmas decorations. Her mom loved to decorate.

"Hey Shorty Bean," her mother called to her. "Would you like to see the Winter Wonderland Show? It starts in ten minutes," she stated as she looked at her watch.

Shorty nodded as her mother got in line to purchase tickets.

"You're just in time," her mom said as her dad walked up to the counter.

"What on earth? More Christmas decorations? It looks like you bought out all the stores!" her dad complained.

"I was just getting us tickets for the Winter Wonderland Show," Shorty's mom said ignoring Dad's jibe. "Would you like to watch it with us? It sounds like someone needs to get into the Christmas spirit doesn't it Shorty?"

Shorty's dad placed his hands on his head and mumbled under his breath, "I'll give you Christmas Spirit," Shorty Bean and her mom burst out in laughter.

She knew her dad was only playing, well mostly playing! It always did take him a little while to get into the holiday season!

"Oh hush now," Shorty's mom scolded. "Would you please take our bags and lock them in the car for us so we can go to the show?" Her mother passed her shopping bags to Dad. He was pretty loaded down as he headed toward the parking lot to put them in the car. While her mother waited for dad to return, Shorty Bean and Smarty began running through the streets of the Wonderland. There were decorated with red and white striped candy canes and Christmas lights. There was a purple velvet carpet with gold tassels that lined the streets and they followed its path. There were many displays and booths to enjoy each one depicting a different country or location around the world. Some were decorated with electric trains, some with brightly colored lights and tinsel, and one had angels with golden wings. Smarty liked the one that had teddy bears in every color imaginable. Another one used numerous candies and ornaments along with animated characters to create ginger bread houses that were as tall as she was! Christmas was not just about presents and candy. It was about the birth of a royal King. It was fun to see how countries around the world celebrated it differently through their displays.

Shorty Bean stopped abruptly as one display caught her eye. It was quite unusual. It was an extraordinary island which was surrounded by crystal blue waters cascading from the very top to a peaceful lake below. On the island there were many elves. Some were sunbathing, while others were building sand castles shaped like Christmas trees. They were all wearing orange shorts and drinking lemonade.

"What a funny display," Shorty Bean remarked to Smarty. It's so odd, I don't know why it draws me so," she declared.

"That gives a whole new meaning to 'fun in the sun'!" Norm exclaimed. Smarty chuckled. Norm wasn't that bad after all. He could be annoying, but he was growing on Smarty, literally. Suddenly within the display Shorty saw a glimpse of White Cloud.

"Smarty, do you see what I see?" Shorty asked afraid to take her eyes off the spot where she had seen him.

"Yes! I saw it, too!" he told her. But, just as quickly as White Cloud appeared, he disappeared. Shorty Bean held the locket around her neck. It brought her comfort just to hold it and then she realized why.

"It reminds me of White Cloud," Shorty told Smarty as he jumped up into her backpack and snuggled into her neck.

"I'm hungry," her dad declared as they all came upon the same display together.

"Why don't we get some pizza," Shorty's mom suggested.

"Sounds good to me. I could eat a horse!" Dad replied as he led the way to the pizza parlor two doors down. He opened one of the double entrance doors and waited as Shorty Bean and her mother entered. Suddenly Shorty stopped still as she read a sign posted on the other door.

No Rats Allowed. "Well, finally, a sign that makes some sense," Shorty's dad said with a laugh.

But Shorty paused before replying, "Well, technically, Smarty is not a rat. He is a ham-dog.

"I'm sorry, honey," her mom interjected. "But you may know that, but others don't. We need to obey the rules for the restaurant. You'll need to take Smarty back to the car until we finish. We can bring him something to eat."

"I'm so sorry, Smarty," Shorty said as she led him back to the car and opened the door. "Why don't you take a nap while we are gone? I'll be sure to bring you some melted cheese and burnt pepperoni just like you like," she said as she closed the door. Smarty pressed his little paw against the car window as Shorty turned to go. The look on his face almost broke her heart. It's not fun to be excluded from something just because of the way you look or who or what you are.

"Everyone is special," Shorty said out loud frustrated with a situation she couldn't change. But she would make it up to Smarty! She walked back to the pizza place quickly and found the table where her mom and dad were already seated.

"We just ordered," her mom informed her as she patted her hand. "I'm really sorry that Smarty couldn't join us." Back at the car, Norm and Smarty were having their own conversation.

"Now you know what it feels like. No one ever wants to be around me," Norm stated as he waved his antennas back and forth and burrowed into Smarty's fur.

"Well, it looks like, it's just you and me," Smarty agreed.

Smarty tried to think of something encouraging to say to Norm. He scratched his head, but nothing came to his mind now. Then he responded, "It's true, no one really likes ticks, but I think your pretty cool!"

Norm mimicked him. "I think your pretty cool!"

"Ok, I take that back. You're annoying. Quit repeating everything I say," Smarty growled at him.

Norm was silent. He didn't want to be annoying. He is tried to find some radio air waves with his antennas. Maybe some nice holiday music could help restore the peace.

*   *   *

"It's okay, Mom. Thanks for understanding," Shorty Bean said as she took a slice of the gooey cheese pizza the waitress had just delivered to their table.

"Well, if you ask me, rats don't belong in a restaurant, just like they don't belong in our beds," her Dad insisted giving Shorty that, "I told you so," look.

"Hey Dad, look over there just outside the window. Is that a reindeer?"

As he turned his head to look out the window where Shorty had indicated, she quickly placed a piece of pizza in a napkin and stuffed it in her backpack.

"Where? I do not see any such thing," her dad responded. "Okay, so, you got me this time. You just wait," he laughed. Shorty Bean just smiled as she finished zipping the backpack closed.

"Well, I'm done shopping. How about you guys? Shall we head home? It's Christmas Eve after all and I still have some things to get ready at home," Shorty's mom announced.

Shorty's dad paid the bill and all three walked back to the car. Smarty was certainly glad to see them. He had been lonely. Shorty unzipped the backpack and motioned for Smarty to crawl inside. It didn't take but a minute for him to smell the pizza and he scurried in for his lunch.

"Shhhh!" Shorty whispered as he snorted with almost every bite. She poked the backpack to get him to be quiet, but he only got louder. Smarty really *loved* pizza! He ate so fast his snorting turned to hiccups! She gave a small pepperoni to Norm and watched as he devoured it like a ravishing beast. "I guess you like pepperoni as much as Smarty does, Norm," Shorty whispered.

"Shorty, make that rat shut up!" her dad said with a stern voice. Just then, Norm's antenna made a piercing sound. There must have been a crossed signal. "What on earth is that sound? It's killing my ears!" Shorty's dad said as he tried to cover his ears with his hands. Norm shook his head and the noise settled, but then it returned and grew loud again.

"There it is again! "he exclaimed.

Shorty wondered if her dad would ever come to like her beloved Smarty! And she was scared he would discover Norm. That wouldn't be good. Dad didn't like rats, but he absolutely hated ticks. One year he was camping and was bitten by one. Ticks can carry various diseases. No, her dad would not be happy if he discovered Norm was living on Smarty!

When they pulled back into the driveway of the cottage, Grandpa Andy stood up and waved. He and Grandma Ellie had been sitting outside on the porch in the rockers, waiting for their return. It was too quiet in the house they decided and went to their favorite spot on the front porch to wait.

As they walked up onto the porch, Grandpa Andy gave them each a hug and declared, "How about if I make us a fire in the fireplace?"

"And I'll make some hot tea and milk," Grandma Ellie declared as she stood up to go with him.

The fire cast a warm glow around the room as Shorty took in the scene. The Christmas tree sparkled with lights and ornaments and the gifts were wrapped and waiting for the next morning. Her parents and grandparents were playing a card game at the table and still munching on warm cookies her grandmother had made for dessert after a heavenly meal. Shorty stretched her arms in the air as a yawn escaped.

"Goodnight, everyone. I'm going to head to bed now. Come on, Smarty, it's time for bed," she coaxed. He was all curled up in his chair that Grandpa Andy made for him. He opened his eyes at the sound of her voice, got up and stretched. "Goodnight everyone," he said automatically.

Shorty's eyes grew wide. No one knew Smarty could talk!

"What said that?" Grandpa Andy inquired.

"Come on, Smarty, it's time for bed," Shorty Bean said ignoring her grandfather's question.

Then she heard the sentence repeated. "Norm!" Shorty Bean thought as her eyes grew big.

"Who is Norm? Grandpa Andy asked.

Smarty put his head down and remained silent.

"Whew! That was close," Shorty declared as she got ready for bed. She wasn't mad at Smarty for talking. In fact, she was too excited to be mad. Tomorrow was her birthday and Jesus' birthday and she knew they were going to have quite the celebration!

"Goodnight," Shorty Bean called out.

"Goodnight," came the reply. Shorty knew it was Norm, but couldn't figure out if he was replying to her or just mimicking her!

"You know, Smarty. Ticks don't live long," Norm informed him.

"Really?" Smarty questioned, not sure if Norm was being serious or not.

"Yes, really," Norm said softly

Smarty thought about what Norm said.

"Well, maybe you're not so bad after all," Smarty concluded. "That is if you would quit making me itch so much!"

"Hey, whatever you say," Norm told him.

"Whatever, is right!" Smarty declared. He would show him who was boss! Until he fell asleep, Smarty's tail kept hitting Norm's antennas. It didn't feel very good and Norm continued to feel sorry for himself and his short lifespan.

"Well, you are probably right, but I've heard that ticks that eat bacon, *really* don't live long!" Smarty joked. He wanted to cheer Norm up.

Smarty couldn't see it, but Norm cracked a small smile before he fell asleep. Mission accomplished!

Chapter Fourteen

Caves of Rain

Shorty Bean was suddenly wide awake. "Do you hear that, Smarty?" she asked as she nudged him awake. It was a strange sound resonating from the rooftop. Her mind started racing. It *was* Christmas after all. Could it be???

She and Smarty raced up the ladder to the attic and opened the window that led to the roof, but it wasn't a sleigh and reindeer on their roof. A brilliant light was emanating off White Cloud. She hadn't found him. He had found her. He looked majestic and strong and motioned for Shorty to join him. She stepped out onto the gently sloped roof and walked up to him. He was smiling.

"Would you like a ride?" he asked as he shook the snow from his wings stretching them to full length.

"Yes, please!" Shorty Bean said as she climbed up on his back. "Come on, Smarty! Let's go," she motioned. Smarty dove into the backpack, but then popped his head out for the perfect view. Norm, unwilling to miss the adventure, had his head up and his antenna's stuck straight up into the air. The signal coming from his antennas had never been so clear. He was in tick heaven.

"Smarty, fear will always keep you from fulfilling your purpose. You must choose to conquer it, or it will conquer you," White Cloud said gently but firmly.

Smarty took a deep breath and then climbed up on White Cloud's back. He snuggled up in front of Shorty so her body could help shield him from the wind. The next thing they both knew, they were soaring in the air.

Although the air was frosty cold, the warmth from White Cloud's body made both Shorty and Smarty feel warm. He glided effortlessly through the air and she could feel the strength of his muscles. He was magnificent and fearless and just being with him made her fearless. They flew through a massive constellation of stars. Shorty Bean reached out her hand to try and touch one, but each time she was just about to succeed, White Cloud swerved. Although she could not see his face, she could feel him chuckle. "Each star has its place in the constellation, Shorty Bean, just as each person has their special place in life. Do not disturb them for as they shine in their place, it makes a beautiful picture. Does it not? So, it is with your life Shorty Bean. You are to let your light shine."

As they reached the forest, White Cloud flew them up to the mountain top where the Coin of Fire had been lost in the river the previous summer.

"Prepare for landing!" White Cloud stated as he glided to a stop on the snowy crag.

Shorty and Smarty slid off his back and looked out over the forest. Immediately White Cloud lifted off and flew into the clouds. As he disappeared into the night, his voice thundered through the air. "Seek and you will find."

"Well, are you ready?" Shorty said as she turned to head down the mountain.

"Ready, for what?" Smarty asked. He wasn't sure he was ready for anything at all and was trying his best to conquer the fear that was trying to creep back in his heart.

"Are you ready to jump?" Shorty said with a laugh.

"Jump off this mountain? Are you nuts?" Smarty responded.

"Look, the locket is glowing, Smarty. White Cloud brought us here, so we could find the Coin of Fire. I know he did. And I know the fastest way off this mountain is to jump. I know it sounds crazy, but I feel like that's what we are supposed to do. Do you believe?"

Smarty gave a small nod in affirmation. He was trying hard to believe.

"Okay on the count of three. One, two, and three!" Shorty shouted as they grabbed hands and jumped together. They found themselves tumbling down a gigantic frozen water slide. With the wind blowing in her face, Shorty held onto Smarty as they sped down the mountainside eventually landing in the snowy bank at the end of the slide. "Whew! Just a few more feet and we would have been sliding across the frozen water!" Shorty said. She walked up to the lake and tapped it with her toes. Frozen solid. She looked around to gather in their surroundings. As she looked beyond the river, she noticed what looked like the mouth of a cave.

Just then, she remembered what Smarty said to her the first time he was able to talk, "We must go back to the Gazman Forest and the Caves of Rain." Could this be the place? She thought.

"Let's go ice-skating, Smarty!" she said as she reached up to one of the pine trees and broke off two long icicles. She laid them against the bottom of her boots to form ice skates. The two glided out on the ice where they begin twirling and dancing. What a performance! Norm stood up on his tiptoes until he could feel the wind. He hung on tight and to enjoy the ride.

Shorty Bean took Smarty's hand and they started to make figure eights. They twirled in unison. Smarty skated under Shorty's legs and around in circles. They were so immersed in their skating that they had forgotten all about the Coin of Fire until they skated over an area of ice that began to flash a bright orange. As it did, Shorty Bean's locket around her neck illuminated.

"Smarty! It must be the Coin of Fire," Shorty shouted. The locket around her neck had opened and the treasure map appeared activated by her faith. On the map was a circle key. Intrigued, Shorty gazed upon the map where a beam of light rose above the Caves of Rain. The light revealed a tall crystal blue waterfall. The water was completely frozen in a cascading motion. It was beautiful.

Shorty looked with wonder as they walked underneath the waterfall to the entrance of a white crystal rock cave. Greeting them at the entrance was a canopy of ghostly white trees. Their branches intertwined to form a narrow passageway inside the cave. As they ventured further inside, Shorty noticed a large tree stump enclosed within a chunk of ice. The key was frozen inside.

"This is it, this is the place!" Smarty exclaimed.

"Come on Smarty. We have to thaw the ice so we can get it out," Shorty told him as they began blowing frozen mass surrounding the stump. Their warm breath had its effect as the ice began to melt. They continued until Shorty was able to reach the key. She tried with all her might to pull it out from the stump, but the key was frozen in place. All she could do was turn it counterclockwise. They heard a clicking sound and then it stopped. She looked around expectantly, but all was still. "I wonder if we did something wrong," Shorty thought. But she had spoken too soon. The ground underneath them began to shake as the Coin of Fire soared up into the air like a blast from a volcano. The locket around her neck opened and the Coin of Fire came to rest safely in its chamber.

"We have them all now, Smarty!" Shorty declared. "It's complete!" Shorty said as she snapped the locket closed. The ground continued to rumble as the power from the unified coins started the domino effect to unravel the mystery. Stars began to fall from the sky and hit the ground around them like grenades.

"Smarty, we have to get out of here," Shorty yelled as she grabbed hold of his hand. But it was as if their feet were glued to the ground. They couldn't move.

Shorty watched in horror as the sky opened. Thunder so loud and strong shook their bodies followed by bolts of lightning that crashed all around them.

The ground beneath them began to rise as the inner core of the earth opened. Smarty and Shorty Bean were suspended in air as if standing on a clear sheet of ice. They could see what looked like a lake of molten lava bubbling beneath them. Between them was a cloud of blackness which reminded Shorty Bean of the Black Bears and their menacing presence. The cloud moved toward the east twirling slowly in a circular formation. Shorty could barely breathe as she watched it happen around her. And her heart pounded so fast, she thought it would burst from her chest. She watched as tortured creatures flew below them. They were crying out in agony.

"Smarty what is this? What are they? They sound so desperate! I can't stand to hear their cries," Shorty said as she put her hands over her ears. Without warning, a spirit force out of nowhere grabbed Shorty's leg and began to pull them down into the blackness. For Shorty it was like being pulled along on a rope. She had absolutely no power to slow their descent until a bright flash of light from the locket created a barrier preventing the force from taking the further. With a loud cry it released its hold and disappeared. As it did, the earth closed and the lava lake disappeared along with the creatures.

Now there was nothing but darkness and silence.

Chapter Fifteen

The Path is Clear

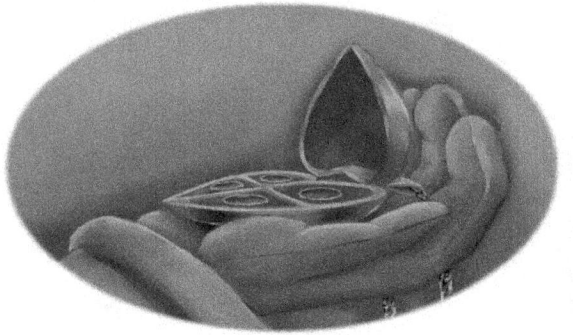

Shorty was ready to cry. Why would White Cloud leave them in such a dangerous place? "I don't know what to do, Smarty," she said as her voice trembled. Just as she was about to give up hope, a walkway made of gold silk appeared above them. It provided a path between the mountains as rays of light radiated from the sky causing the darkness to fade. Two massive white wolves with wings descended from the light rays. They picked up Shorty Bean and Smarty and carried them up to the place of light.

As the wolves deposited them gently on firm footing, Shorty realized they were standing before White Cloud. An unusual crowd of forest animals were around him. Shorty shook her head to make sense of it all. There must have been thousands of creatures there together, but they were at peace with each other. Lions wrestled in play with blue birds. She saw an orange elephant frolicking with a green mouse and a black rabbit sat on top of a spotted tiger's stomach as he read him a book! It was unbelievable. "Is this place real?" Shorty Bean asked.

But the most amazing site of all was a throne made of one gigantic sapphire. Imbedded in it were jewels in every color of the rainbow. "I've never seen anything so beautiful," she declared in awe.

As she and Smarty watched, a scroll was opened by two eloquent grey owls. They began calling a list of names out loud.

"Whose names are you reading?" Shorty asked.

"We are reading the names of those who will live in the place of light," they replied.

"Can we live in the place of light?" Shorty asked.

"Yes," they replied. "Your name is Shorty Bean and your friend is Smarty, both of your names

are written here in the book."

"How did we get our names written in the book?" they asked curiously although they were both relieved to hear that they were included.

"Your names were written once you believed," the owls responded.

White Cloud was standing beside them listening silently, but now he spoke. "Do you believe in me, Shorty Bean?"

"Yes, I do!" she replied without hesitation. He turned to Smarty next. Smarty's tail was tucked between his legs. He was trying hard to be brave.

"Smarty, do you believe in me?" White Cloud asked.

"Yes, I do," Smarty stuttered.

"Then come to my right side," he instructed. Smarty stepped forward and stood next to White Cloud. Just then the Black Bears appeared out of nowhere. Smarty trembled as their low menacing growls rumbled in their throats.

"Do you believe in me?" White Cloud asked each bear separately.

Growling and snarling under their breath, they responded in unison, "We don't believe in you and we never will," they sneer as they show their sharp teeth.

The sky rumbled with thunder as White Cloud pronounced judgement, "Seize them. Forever they will be in darkness!" he exclaimed. Two white wolves with great power stepped forward and hurled the bears down from the place of light. Smarty watched as the earth opened once again, and the river of molten lava appeared to swallow the bears. Black Ravens appeared next and circled above the lake of lava. Their eyes were a brilliant red which gave an eerie glow in the darkness.

"There is a great divide which I have placed between these two places. The darkness cannot travel here, nor can the light travel there," White Cloud explained. Shorty looked at him as he spoke trying to understand. His face appeared sad as he spoke.

They had seen so much that didn't make sense. But White Cloud had one more thing for Shorty and Smarty.

Chapter Sixteen

The Diamond in the Deep

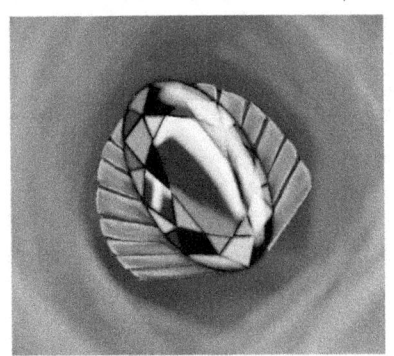

"What would you like me to show you? You can see anything you wish" White Cloud said as he motioned for them to climb back up on his back. It was time to leave.

"You mean, we can see anything?" Shorty questioned? "If so, I want to fly in the deep ocean."

"As you wish, climb aboard," he responded as he bent down ever so slightly so Shorty Bean could climb on his back.

"What about me?" Smarty asked.

"We could not forget about you," Shorty replied as she held out her hand for him to grab. As he took hold, she pulled him up onto White Cloud's back and nestled him close to her as the majestic eagle took off.

They flew over the ocean and circled twice before he dove into the water below. For an instant, Shorty wondered if they would drown, but once underneath, a new world was unveiled before their eyes. The water wasn't thick, but almost transparent and they both could breathe without difficulty. It was amazing. Norm was wide-eyed and silent for the first time. He was having the time of his life!

As White Cloud soared through the water they could see vivacious rocks, bizarre fish, and other oceanic creatures. In the distance, a seashell that glittered brightly was shining on the ocean floor.

"It looks like a diamond; can we go see it?" Shorty asked.

White Cloud set his retraceable lens on the shimmering light. (This was something he used when he needed to see across far distances.) With the destination targeted, in a heartbeat, they reached the sandy bottom. Shorty and Smarty gently glided off his back and walked over to the glittering rock. It *was* a diamond. Shorty picked it up and placed it in the backpack. As she zipped her bag closed she realized that the water was settling, and an underground city appeared.

"What is that?" she asked him.

But rather than answering, White Cloud expanded his wings and blocked the city from their view. "It's time to go back to the surface, you've seen enough in the waters," he stated.

"Ok, let's go, Come on, Smarty." Shorty Bean said as they climbed up on his back. "Do we have to go back to the cottage?" Shorty asks.

"Yes, it is time to go, back," White Cloud replied.

"But, I want to stay with you," Shorty pleaded.

White Cloud's voice dropped down to a whisper, "There, there, my love. All is well. When you return you will fall into a deep sleep. These things you have seen will not frighten you, but will be tucked into your memory for when you need them. They are a vision of things to come."

"Merry Christmas, Shorty Bean and Happy Birthday!"

Shorty's eyes popped open at the sound of many voices. She smiled as saw her mom and dad and Grandpa Andy and Grandma Ellie all smiling at her. Mrs. Patty and her kids were even there to wish her a happy birthday.

"Happy Birthday to you, Happy Birthday to you, Happy Birthday, Dear Shorty, Happy Birthday to you!" they sang.

"Make a wish, Shorty," Grandpa Andy instructed her as Grandma Ellie held out a beautiful pink birthday cake she had baked the night before. Shorty closed her eyes, made a wish, and blew out seven candles.

"Open my present first," Smarty said impatiently. "Open mine, please, open mine,"

"Ok, I will," she replied as she took the small package from before her. She pulled off the paper to reveal a small framed picture. It was Smarty in outer space. "Where did this come from?" she whispered.

"It is from Tripod He took it when I blew into the sky after drinking the serum. It's quite funny don't you think? But trust me, that box turtle is up to something in outer space," Smarty informed her with a wink.

"Well Shorty, open ours next," her mother said. Shorty wasn't one to gently unwrap a gift and save the paper. She tore off the ribbon and paper to reveal a new hat and scarf.

"I love it! Thank you," she exclaimed.

"I seem to have one more gift over here," Grandpa Andy said with a sly smile. Shorty Bean grinned as she opened her gift from her grandparents.

"My very own tea cup, with pink roses! Thank you, Grandpa and Grandma!"

"You're welcome. Now you will have a special cup when you come to visit again!" he explained.

"Okay, get dressed birthday girl. We are going downstairs and we will have breakfast and then open Christmas presents. Hurry," her mom instructed. After they had all left the room, Smarty crawled over to where Shorty Bean still sat on the bed.

"Where is your locket?" he asked.

"It is on the bedside table where I always leave it," she replied. "Oh, we must go and see White Cloud!" she exclaimed as the locket reminded her of her assignment.

"We already did. Don't you remember?" Smarty asked rather confused.

"No, I don't remember anything," Shorty told him.

"Are you serious? You do not remember anything?" he questioned. Surely, she was joking. But he could tell by the confused look on Shorty's face, that she indeed did not remember the events of the night before. Or did she? Resting on her dresser, Shorty noticed one more present. It was beautifully wrapped in royal blue paper with a silver bow.

"Hmmm. I wonder who this is from," she said to herself as she read the note attached.

Seek and you will find. With love, Grandma Ellie.

Shorty's fingers trembled as she opened the gift. One by one she pulled out piece after piece of intricately hand-sewn patchwork squares. Each one depicted a different adventure from their journey in the forest.

"Look this one is of Ms. Nora when she danced a jig with her broom. And here's one, Smarty, where you're running down the pathway. And here we are ice-skating. A look of confusion crossed her face. It was then Norm tuned in his antennas and they began to go berserk. Then Smarty and Shorty heard the voice of White Cloud repeating what he said the night he dropped them off at the cottage.

"There, there, my love. All is well. When you return you will fall into a deep sleep. These things you have seen will not frighten you, but will be tucked into your memory for when you need them. They are a vision of things come." Immediately Shorty Bean recollected a part of the journey.

"The Caves of Rain," she said softly.

As Shorty picked up the last patch she looked at Smarty with a questioning look, "In this one we are in the ocean with White Cloud. Smarty, were we in the ocean with White Cloud?"

Before Smarty could answer, the locket on the bedside began to glow and vibrate.

"The sea shell diamond, I remember now," Shorty said. The power of the locket helped her, once again. She jumped off the bed and grabbed her backpack. But when she opened the pouch it was empty. "The diamond is gone!" Shorty wailed. "Where can it be?"

Frantically, she and Smarty checked every place they could imagine, but there was no diamond. "I must have lost it! Oh, no!" she cried.

"We will find it," Smarty tried to reassure his friend, but it was no use. Big tears began to form and trickled down her face. "Listen to me. All we have to do is ask White Cloud where it is the next time we see him. He helped us find the Coin of Fire. I know he'll help you find it," he said with confidence.

Just then Grandpa Andy opened the bedroom door. "Aren't you forgetting something?"

"What?" Shorty asked.

"Did you forget what day it is?" he said with a smile.

"Christmas!" Shorty Bean yelled as she and Smarty leapt out of bed and dashed down the stairs. "Merry Christmas to everyone!" Shorty exclaimed as she started to hand out the presents she had wrapped for her family.

They all watched and laughed as Shorty Bean dove to retrieve her presents buried underneath the tree. "Smarty stop that!" Shorty laughed as she pulled some wrapping paper out of his mouth. "You shouldn't eat wrapping paper! Oh, but we forgot to eat breakfast, didn't we?" she laughed again. Smarty hated to miss meals.

What a glorious Christmas morning! "This is the best day ever!" Shorty Bean declared after all the presents had been opened and they were seated at the table. Smarty nodded.

It didn't seem like life could get any better. She had a warm, cozy home, a loving family and they were all gathered together.

"Who will say prayer before we eat?" her mother asked.

"I will," Shorty Bean volunteered. She had much for which to be thankful.

Chapter Seventeen

Never say Goodbye

S horty let out a contented sigh as she snuggled next to Grandma Ellie in front of the fireplace that night. "Thank you for the patches, Grandma."

Somehow, Grandma Ellie always knew about their excellent adventures. "You're welcome, dear," Grandma Ellie replied as she gave her granddaughter a hug.

"So how did you know about the forest?" Shorty asked as she looked up at her.

"Oh, grandmothers know about everything," Grandma Ellie replied with a laugh. Shorty smiled. That seemed about right.

"Will you come back next spring, Shorty Bean? I could use your help in the garden. It needs your hands to work the soil and tend to the roses," Grandpa Andy told her.

Shorty fondly reflected back to the day in the rose garden last summer and nodded, "I cannot wait! I would love to!" She walked over and gave Grandpa Andy a kiss on his cheek as she turned to her mom. "Mom, can I, please?" she begged.

"We'll see," her mom promised as she grabbed Shorty's coat and handed it to her. "It's time to go. Put your coat on and make sure you got everything out of your room," she instructed.

As her Dad pulled the car around front, Shorty Bean and Smarty jumped inside. However, before she shut the door, Grandma Ellie walked over to where they sat and held out both of her hands. They were closed tightly in a fist.

Shorty looked at her with questioning eyes. "Pick one," she instructed.

Shorty pointed with her finger. "This one," she said and then changed her mind. "No, that one."

Grandma Ellie opened her left fist. It was empty. "Nope nothing there," Grandma Ellie chuckled. Shorty pointed to her right hand next. Grandma Ellie opens her right fist and Shorty Bean's eyes lit up with joy. It was her seashell diamond!

"Keep this in a safe place, promise?" Grandma said with a twinkle in her eye.

"Yes, I will, I promise," Shorty replied as Grandma Ellie shut the car door.

"Shorty, I can have a ring made from this seashell to fit your little finger," her dad suggested.

"Yes, I would love that!" she replied as they pulled out of the driveway and headed for home.

Shorty stared out the window on the trip home. There was snow on the ground. She had a seashell diamond in her pocket and her best friend was snuggled beside her. It had been a wonderful Christmas.

Smarty sighed, shook his head, and snuggled deeper in the backpack. "Hey guys, it's time for me to go back into the woods," Norm exclaimed.

"Hey guys, it's time to go back into the woods," Smarty echoed reversing their roles.

With a quick salute, Norm buzzed his antennas and jumped off Smarty's back. He crawled back into the forest. "Farewell!" he yelled.

"Good riddance, Norm." Smarty retorted,

"Don't be mean, Smarty. He's not that bad," Shorty reprimanded him.

"You're right," he agreed as he gave a small wave.

"Farewell, Norm," Shorty Bean said. She had actually grown rather fond of him.

They watched as Norm meandered through the trees and into the woods. He had the time of his life on his adventure with Shorty Bean and Smarty!

Most of the way home in the front seat Shorty's mom and dad reminisced about the holiday. While in the backseat, Shorty Bean and Smarty shared their own stories—and they had many of them. Shorty wiggled her toe feeling her beloved daisy toe ring. Smarty loosened his cape to get comfortable and gave a yawn. He was about ready to nap. Shorty placed her hands around her locket and held it tightly. She wondered what new adventures awaited them when she returned in the spring.

"Smarty, you are my best friend in the whole world," she told him. Smarty nudged her with his nose and fell asleep. Shorty Bean thought also of her grandparents and how much she loved them. It made it extra special that the adventures seemed to always be at their house, but maybe it was because there was so much love there. Just as the locket held power, so does love and no matter how far apart loved ones lived, their love would always be tucked away in her heart.

There were many things Shorty didn't remember about the adventures that night. As White Cloud said, "The mystery revealed was only a vision." The meaning was for another time and she would remember at the proper time when she needed to. For now, Shorty held the locket close to her heart. She closed her eyes and began to dream about their next adventure at her Grandparent's cottage.

About the Author

Holly Szurpicki was born in Detroit, Michigan, the car capital of the world. Although she couldn't drive yet, her imagination had a way of taking her wherever she dreamed to go.

Holly wished one day to be a princess, a park ranger, or an entrepreneur. She states, "Two out of three is not too shabby."

She is passionate about creating stories, screenplays and writing songs. Holly began writing a manuscript in the year 2001 which lay dormant as she focused on raising her two children. But when the year 2008 arrived, she teamed up with a virtual animation studio out of New York. That is when the dream came to life, and the Shorty Bean story became her first novel.

Art and individual creativity have tremendously inspired her throughout her career. Holly possesses visual creativity which takes her to places beyond words to live animation in her mind. Being able to envision her characters and their environments is a true gift, and she recognizes this as supernatural.

Despite many tragic circumstances she has faced throughout her life, Holly has always maintained a positive attitude and loves to encourage others to pursue their God-given dreams.

Her goal for writing children's books is to create a safe and wholesome environment for imagination. Holly desires for children to DREAM BIG, and never forget that there is nothing impossible with God. She believes each one of us has a divine destiny and wants others to never be afraid to pursue their dreams.

Holly lives in northern Minnesota with her husband and two children and a water dog named Klause. She loves the outdoors, photography and fishing to name a few of her passions.

For more information regarding the Shorty Bean series,
future works or general inquiries,
check out her website:
www.hollykszurpicki.com.

www.ingramcontent.com/pod-product-compliance
Lightning Source LLC
Chambersburg PA
CBHW071343170626
46811CB00003B/962